Also by Traci L. Jones

Standing Against the Wind

FiNDiNG
MY PLACE

FINDING MY PLACE

Traci L. Jones

Farrar Straus Giroux ✷ New York

www.fsgteen.com

Library of Congress Cataloging-in-Publication Data
Jones, Traci L.
    Finding my place / Traci L. Jones.— 1st ed.
      p.   cm.
    Summary: After moving to an affluent suburb of Denver in 1975, ninth-grader
Tiphanie feels lonely at her nearly all-white high school until she befriends another
"outsider" and discovers that prejudice exists in many forms.
    ISBN: 978-0-374-33573-1
    [1. African Americans—Colorado—Denver—History—20th century—Juvenile
fiction.   2. African Americans—Fiction.   3. Prejudices—Fiction.   4. Race
relations—Fiction.   5. Moving, Household—Fiction.   6. Friendship—Fiction.
7. High schools—Fiction.   8. Schools—Fiction.   9. Denver (Colo.)—History—
20th century—Fiction.]   I. Title.

PZ7.J72752 Fi 2010
[Fic]—dc22

                                                                    2008054433

*For all those African American
young ladies out there who are trying
to find their place as the only ones*

Acknowledgments

A special thanks to . . .

Beverly Reingold for believing that the convoluted mess of a manuscript I sent her could be turned into a readable book, and

Lisa Graff for proving that it could.

Lisa Cobb, Helen Matthews, and Jackie Turner for being my friends, fellow writers, sounding boards, and first draft critics, and

Mom, Dad, Peter, and Regina for never doubting me for a minute even when I gave them ample reason to, and

Desiree, Andrew, Isaiah, and Brooke for being my beautiful babies, and

always, Tony, for being the alpha and omega of my love.

FiNDiNG
MY PLACE

The Talented Tenth Lecture

Your mother and I know switching schools is hard, Tiphanie, but we're sure you'll excel like you always have. At your old school you did well, and we are proud of you, but you can't simply do well at your new school. You must do superbly. You will have to work twice as hard as your white classmates. You will have to be twice as polite, twice as obedient, and twice as studious just to get good grades. In order to get great grades you must make no mistakes. You have to be better just to be equal. Everyone around will be watching and judging us, Tiphanie.

Remember the "Talented Tenth," Tiphanie? DuBois was thinking about you when he wrote that essay. You are one of the best of our race, part of the talented tenth that will elevate us to the next level. Never shirk your duties. You are not only representing our family, but Afro-Americans everywhere. We know you can handle it. You'll make us proud like you always have. This is the kind of opportunity your mother and I, and so many others, fought for in the move-ment, so don't squander it. Don't worry, you'll find your place here.

Now, have a great day and come home immediately after school and clean that pigsty of a bedroom.

For most people, the big news during the fall of 1975 was the second assassination attempt on President Ford. Not for me. For me, that October was the month my father, Morris Ray Baker, and my mother, Annie Louise Baker, decided to completely ruin my life. Oh, they claimed it was not only a good move for our family, but a step forward for our race as a whole. My parents were *big* on doing their part to uplift the race, which meant I was expected to do my part as well. And I didn't usually mind, because most of the time it was easy stuff, like making good grades and not getting in trouble at school. Sometimes, not often, but *sometimes*, it was even fun, like going out of town to Afro-American arts festivals.

But this time my parents went too far—they made us move. To the suburbs of all places! As if living in Denver, Colorado, wasn't bad enough. Being from Colorado got you no clout from other Blacks—especially the ones from D.C., Atlanta, or Chicago. But at least before we moved I was in the Blackest part of Colorado there was—the neighborhood just northeast of downtown.

Then my father got a promotion which came with a huge raise. While I was happy for my father in a vague *I love my daddy* sort of way, I didn't see how his new job would affect me personally. After all, even though Daddy was the first Black vice president at Colorado National Bank of Denver, I was still expected to clean my room. And when my house-wife mother announced a few weeks later that she had got-ten a job as a real estate broker, I thought, "Cool! Go on with your bad self, Mom!" But I knew I'd still have to listen to my parents' endless lectures. As far as I was concerned, unless the promotion and the new job came with a maid and a pair of earplugs, nothing much would change in my life.

I was wrong. With my parents' new incomes we suddenly had enough money to move out of our small but comfort-able house. This meant that instead of going to high school with the kids—the Black kids—I'd known all my life, I'd be one of two Blacks going to Brent Hills High in Brent Hills, Colorado. I hadn't even had much time to settle into high school in Parkside yet. Five measly weeks. I'd barely learned my locker combination when we up and moved.

The new house was only thirty minutes from our old neighborhood, but it was light-years away from my former life. Oh, my parents told me I'd still see my old friends. They said we'd still go to the same church we'd always gone to, and we would invite my friends from school and church over to the house for slumber parties and stuff. But even at fourteen-and-a-half, I knew that seeing someone once or twice a month, or even every Sunday for a couple of hours, wasn't enough to make a friendship last.

When my mother took me to register for ninth grade at my new high school I was a little stunned by how different my old and new schools were from each other. Brent Hills High looked like a big office building. It was only five or six years old, so it looked shiny and new—in a plastic, fake way. My old school, Grove High, was built way back in the late 1800s and it looked well used but sturdy.

"We are so pleased to have Tip-han-ni here," said the school secretary as she carefully reviewed the stack of forms my mother handed her.

"It's pronounced 'Tiffany,' " replied my mother. "Spelled like Stephanie, except with a *Ti* instead of an *Ste*."

Tiphanie Jayne Baker. My parents were generally conservative and old-fashioned, but they were on the cutting edge of at least one Black cultural idiosyncrasy—they were the first in the growing wave of Black mothers and fathers to be overly creative in the choosing and spelling of their children's names. I mean, *they* had normal names, Morris and Annie, both of which, I liked to point out, were extremely easy to spell and *never* got mispronounced.

"Well, isn't that a unique way to spell it?" simpered the secretary, whose name according to her nameplate was Minny Tingle. And *my* name was odd? "It will be so nice to have a diverse student body. You know, while Denver has the population to make busing work, poor little Brent Hills just can't find any Neg . . . umm . . . different people to bring in."

My mother's eyebrows shot up at the secretary's poor choice of words, but she chose to be polite.

"So exactly how many other Blacks attend Brent Hills?" asked my mother, overemphasizing the word *Black* for the secretary's cultural education.

"Well, let's see," Miss Tingle answered. "There's Bradley Jepperson. He's in the ninth grade too. That will give Tiphand . . . er, um, Tifhan . . . your daughter a ready-made friend."

"Tiphanie, it's Tiphanie. The *ph* makes an *f* sound," I interrupted. I didn't want my teachers and my classmates to call me "Tip Hand Nie." Just the thought of that happening annoyed me. As did the assumption that Bradley would be my "ready-made friend." I didn't like all the Blacks in my last school, so what made her think I'd like Bradley? Did she like all the white people she knew?

"Oh, yes, dear, sorry about that. Well, Bradley is the only Neg . . . Black boy here. But we do have several Mexicans, and one little Japanese boy. Or maybe he's Chinese. I can never tell with them."

"I see," my mother said, with more than a tinge of irritation to her voice.

At that moment, I didn't care about the progress of the race or being an upstanding Afro-American citizen. I wanted to be back in Denver, with people who looked like me and understood me and knew how to pronounce my name. And where would I buy stuff to fix my hair way out here? I was miserable before I'd even gone to school one day.

"So exactly how many is 'several Mexicans'?" I asked, as

politely as I could. I figured if there weren't any Blacks around, then hanging out with browns would have to do. I had never had a white friend in my whole life and I was certain that I wouldn't find any here in the 'burbs. And what if this Bradley boy turned out to be an Uncle Tom?

"Why, I believe we have eight," Miss Tingle answered cheerfully. "There are at least five Garcias here. I think they're from the same family." As it turned out, only two of them were related. You'd think that Miss Tingle, working in the school office, would know that.

"So in a school this size, you only have ten students who aren't white?" my mother asked. I saw her glance over at me with a bit of concern. She knew how I was about having friends, and lots of them.

"Oh, no," replied Miss Tingle earnestly. "We have that little Oriental boy."

"Oh, that's right," my mother snapped. "You've almost a full dozen. You're quite the model of a diverse American school."

Miss Tingle beamed up at my mother and said, "Yes, yes we are. Why, I believe that's one percent colored."

2

The night before my first day of school I was in a nervous frenzy. I had several outfits lying on my bed, ranging from ultra casual to church dressy. I'd packed and repacked my backpack about a half dozen times and I couldn't figure out what to do with my hair. Afro or two Afro puffs? Afro bun? I needed help, so I called my best friend, Renee, to debate the virtues of a miniskirt versus hip-huggers, platforms versus clogs.

Renee was silent for a moment. Then she said something that put it all in perspective for me. "It doesn't matter what you wear, or how you do your hair, Tif. You're the only Black girl in the entire school. At best, you can hope for curiosity, at worst, outright hostility. I'd suggest you choose something old and comfortable—you know, something that you won't mind getting ruined, in case of flying food. Then go to sleep. You'll need to be fully rested and on your toes."

"Flying food?" I asked. "What do you mean?"

"You know," Renee said with a don't-be-so-stupid tone to her voice. "Food flying at you. Like your mom and dad at the Woolworth counters down south."

Renee knew all my parents' stories about being a part of the civil rights movement. They'd gone to Lane College in Jackson, Tennessee, in the sixties and they were part of the Woolworth lunch counter sit-ins. After their classes, they would change into their best clothes and go sit at the lunch counter for hours, never being served so much as a glass of water. They talked about how people would accidentally-on-purpose bump into them or spill entire plates of food onto their heads. My parents also told Renee and me about all the rules that had been created for the sit-ins. "Wear your Sunday clothes. No laughing. No talking. Be polite. Don't block the entrances. And don't strike back." That's the one that always gave me chills, thinking how hard it would have been to just sit there while you were yelled and cursed at. To have to walk through groups of mean, angry white people shouting awful things at you, and say nothing back. To have food thrown on your best clothes and sit there pretending that nothing happened. My mother has a small scar from when someone threw a lit cigar at her. That burn is her badge of honor.

All those students who were pelted with food as they sat peacefully at the lunch counters, or the girls and boys who were attacked by police dogs as they marched—it wasn't only very recent history, it was my family's personal legacy. And I was expected to live up to it every day of my life. But while I greatly admired their inner strength, their sense of purpose, and their bravery, I seriously doubted that I possessed any of those things myself. *I* was scared.

That night I dreamed I was surrounded by jeering white faces and pelted with cocktail weenies—my favorite party food used as a weapon against me. Just as I was getting ready to throw the mini hot dogs back at my attackers, my parents appeared and told me that the proper way to respond was not to respond at all.

In the morning I expected a little coddling from my parents, but my father gave me the usual goodbye kiss on the cheek and headed off to work as if it was a normal day. My mother drove me to school but just pulled up in front, saying something about wanting to be early on her first day of work. She could have at least *offered* to walk me up to the door.

"Have a wonderful day, honey," she said.

"Shouldn't you come in with me, maybe, Mom?" I asked, trying not to sound afraid, but hoping she'd notice my fear anyway.

"I wish I had time, sweetie, but I want to be sure to be early today. I need to make a good first impression too, you know. I'm the only Black commercial property salesperson they have. Besides, you're a big girl now, a high schooler. You have your class list right there. And of course, that wonderful brain of yours. Hurry along now. Make us proud."

My mother flashed me a quick smile, then leaned over and gave me a hearty pat on my leg. "Go on. You don't want to be late to your first class, or any of them for that matter. That is a stereotype you are *not* to reinforce. Love you, sweetie."

As I got out of the car, a picture suddenly popped into my head of the Little Rock Nine walking into that all-white high school in Arkansas. They had all looked so brave, staring straight ahead, heads held high, clutching their books to their chests. They had also been protected by national guardsmen. As for me, I was all by myself. That had me pretty scared until I realized that no one was paying any attention to me. So I held my head up and marched toward the front door. No one I passed said a word to me.

My first class was English, which was not my favorite subject—too boring, too wordy, too abstract—but at least I'd get it over with right away. I found my classroom easily and walked inside.

"Hello," the teacher greeted me. "I'm Mrs. Deasy. You must be my new student."

"Yes, ma'am. Tiphanie Baker."

"Well, Miss Tiphanie Baker, pick a seat. We have no assigned seating so anywhere is fine."

I chose the middle row, second seat in. At the warning bell streams of students began to pour in. At first I watched them, but stopped after I got a nasty look from one of them. After that I stared down at my desk instead, wishing I was back at my old school, where at least I would have had desk carvings to read. At Brent Hills all the desks were squeaky clean.

When I glanced up again I noticed that I was in a sea of

empty seats. No one was sitting to my left or my right, behind or in front of me. Looking back down at my desk would let them know I cared how they acted, so I held my head up and stared at the blackboard. As the last bell rang, a white guy with curly brown hair and big brown eyes sat in the empty seat behind me. He gave me a friendly look, but he didn't speak, so neither did I.

I was so busy thinking about the look he'd given me that I almost didn't realize Mrs. Deasy was speaking.

"Tiphanie, do you need supplies?" she asked me.

"Excuse me, ma'am?" My voice sounded timid and meek, not at all normal.

"Pencil and papers," she said gently, as if she were scared of hurting my feelings. "I just asked the class to get them out. Were you able to buy supplies? Do you need some? I always bring a little extra for students who need them."

There was a smattering of titters around the class. Mrs. Deasy gave everyone what she must have believed was a stern look, but it just made her appear startled and frightened.

"Oh, no, ma'am, I've got plenty right here, thank you," I said, a little louder than I meant to. I pulled out my supplies and dropped them on my desk with a loud plop.

In the hallway after English ended, I checked my schedule and saw that my next class was algebra. I loved math. Math was solid and predictable. Plus it came easily for me, *very* easily—but that wasn't why I liked it. I liked it because it was something I could count on—$1 + 1$ would always equal 2, just like x in the equation $12x - 10 = 2x + 10$ would always equal 2. How could you not appreciate that? I headed to my locker to dig out my math book.

The Brent Hills hallways were as chaotic as the ones at my old school, so dodging the crowds of loud, laughing kids should have felt normal for me. But that first day it felt anything but normal. I had never felt so Black—and so friendless—in my entire life. Where were those Mexican kids anyway? And that Black guy?

As I was trying to find my classroom, this boy with a big, square head and a blond crew cut bumped right into me and knocked my books out of my hands. He didn't even say "Excuse me." My things landed right in front of another kid who looked at the mess, looked at me, and then stepped over it.

I got to class and instead of plopping down in any random chair I gave my desk selection a little more thought—hoping to avoid the same sea of empty seats. This time I picked the first chair in the last row, but before I knew it I found myself in a sea of blond girls who talked around me as if I wasn't there. A little black speck in an ocean of yellow.

My math teacher, Mr. Ash, was young, and had hair so long I was surprised Brent Hills had even hired him. It almost touched his collar! He looked just like that Warren Beatty guy from the movie *Shampoo*, which my parents hadn't let me see because it was R-rated.

We started class by doing a few quadratic equations at our seats. Piece of cake. When Mr. Ash asked for volunteers to solve some problems on the chalkboard, my hand went up as if it had a mind of its own. Math did that to me. When it turned out I was the only one who had gotten my problem right, Mr. Ash asked me if I could explain to the class why the other problems were wrong. Sho 'nuff I could.

Any subject after math had to be a letdown. U.S. history, French 1A, blah, blah, blah. The only highlight during those two hours was that I finally saw a couple of Mexican guys on my way to French class. They looked at me with friendly smiles but continued talking to each other in Spanish. Just as I was wishing I'd signed up for Spanish instead of French, the blockhead guy who'd run into me that morning plowed into me again, and this time I was sure it was on purpose. He even looked back and snickered at me before walking away. I didn't know who he was, but I hated him already.

Even though I was starving by lunchtime, I still dreaded going into the cafeteria. Lunch was the most important time of the day—not because of the food, but because of the socializing. If I'd been back at my old school, Renee and I would be heading for the front of the cafeteria, where there were three small square tables pushed together. That was *the* table—full of freshman jocks, student council members, and cool, smart kids like me. My friends.

That first day at Brent Hills, instead of being surrounded by my home slices, I was standing alone, holding my tray like a life preserver, trying to figure out my options. Out of the corner of my eye, I saw the blockhead heading my way. He was flapping his jaw at his friend, and I was tempted to trip him until I heard my parents' voices in my head, and I walked away from him instead.

I sat at the largest table I could find, partly hoping that

someone would have to sit down with me because the other tables had filled up, and partly to be obnoxious and force other people to sit cramped together at a tiny table if they didn't want to sit with me. The guy who'd sat behind me in English headed in my direction. As he walked over my heart gave a little skip. But then he pulled out one of the chairs from my table and carried it away without saying a word.

"I'm fine," I muttered to my sandwich. "Thank you for asking. And how are you?" My bologna didn't answer.

On the way to my locker after lunch, I decided it was time to be bold. Rather than peering past people, I decided to look right in their faces. I met the eyes of a few. Some looked away quickly, others gazed back blankly, and some stared at me curiously. But no one spoke, and neither did I.

My next class was gym, where we had to pair up and— surprise, surprise—I was the one left with the scary gym teacher. When that horror was over, I gave a silent prayer of thanks because I only had two classes left until I could go home. But when I walked in to physical science 2X my heart sank a little because the room was filled with lab tables that seated two. I sat at the table directly in front of the teacher, Mr. Wells, another young guy, who smiled at me. I smiled back gratefully and then busied myself with pulling out my notebooks, not expecting anyone to sit down next to me. No one did.

At last it was my final period of the day, home economics. I was irritated just walking to that class. I had told my mother repeatedly that I did not need to learn how to sew and to cook, but she had lectured me about the importance of learning something she called "life skills" and signed me up anyway. Ugh.

On my way there, a girl burst out of the door of a nearby classroom, joking and tussling with some boy, and bumped right into me. She squealed in surprise and twisted away from me as if by merely touching me she'd gotten burned.

Home economics was filled with the same group of blondes that had been in my algebra class. In fact, they seemed to have multiplied. The whole class was made up of a bunch of blondes, a few Mexican girls, and me. I sat down next to one of the less-popular-looking blondes, a ratty white girl dressed like a sixties hippy. For some strange reason she was chewing on her hair.

The teacher spent the first twenty minutes of class explaining our new sewing unit. Twenty minutes of talking about learning how to hem, miter, and topstitch. I wanted someone to kill me right then. As the teacher launched into her inspired idea about doing a brief section devoted to cleaning later in the semester, I heard a voice whisper loudly behind me.

"I won't be doing any cleaning. I'll just hire her to do it. It's not like she'll grow up to be anything but a maid anyway. Lord knows she probably needs the money too."

I turned and saw several of the blondes laughing and twittering, looking over in my direction. I narrowed my eyes, but when they seemed surprised that I was glaring at them, I immediately felt a twinge of uncertainty and spun back around. Maybe they were talking about the ratty girl next to me. She looked upset, and clearly she was an outsider too. That, however, didn't make me feel any better.

At last, the final bell rang and I was free to go home. I waded like a fish swimming upstream through the students who were standing around talking with friends. No one jeered or threw things at me, and I guess I couldn't ask for much more than that—except maybe a "Hi" or the occasional "Excuse me."

That would have been real nice.

3

It wasn't until I got home, anxious to be able to talk to someone after a day of silence, that I remembered I was on my own for the next couple of hours. Mom was at work, which meant there was no one to fix my snack, and no one to talk to about my day. For a minute I felt a flash of anger. Why couldn't she have waited a week before starting her new job? This uplifting-the-race stuff was cramping my style.

I wandered into the kitchen and pulled out a package of Oreos and poured a glass of milk. "Ha!" I announced to the empty kitchen. "I can have as many cookies as I want, so there! And I can watch television before I start my homework too." I felt a little silly talking to our new olive green kitchen appliances, but it felt good to finally hear my own voice again. I decided I needed to call Renee.

When her mother answered, she told me Renee wasn't home yet. I glanced at the clock. It was 2:50. Renee had probably stopped by Brooks' Corner Market and was hanging out with all the other kids, buying Icees and chips. A pang of homesickness hit me and I pushed my plate of cookies away. Suddenly I wasn't hungry anymore. I tried calling my other friends, but no one else had made it home yet either. They were all probably together, having a blast.

I made my way to the den, sat down, and turned on the TV, but watching *Gilligan's Island* and *I Dream of Jeannie* reruns all alone wasn't appealing. I gave up my rebellion and started on my homework.

When my mother walked in an hour later, she was so excited about her first day at work that she forgot to ask me how school was.

"You would not believe my day, baby girl!" she said, pulling out a box of Hamburger Helper. "You remember this past Sunday at church Mr. Casey was talking about the oil company he works for and how they're expanding and need new office space? Well, this morning the first thing I did after getting introduced to everyone at the office was call him up. And the next thing I know I have a new client. In fact, after only two hours at work I have the biggest client in the office! I'm the most popular employee there! I've got lunch dates for the next two weeks. The people in the office are all so nice, and really eager to do business with me. They realize I can open up a whole new client base to them. I love it! The only color that matters in business is green!"

"That's cool, Mom," I muttered. "I'm glad *you* made friends on your first day."

I guess that got my mother's attention, because she finally asked, "So how was your day, sweetie? Any problems? Did you get lost? Were your classes too hard?"

"No, I didn't get lost, and my classes were fine," I said. "It's the same as Grove. Well, except for the fact that I have zero friends."

"Oh, sweetie, that's just because they haven't gotten to know you yet, that's all. They didn't say anything to you that made you uncomfortable, did they?"

"No, but—" I started.

"They didn't harass you, did they?"

"No, but—"

"They didn't throw things at you or threaten you or anything like that, did they?"

"No, they didn't, it's just that—"

"Well, sweetie, remember, you're the new kid, that's all. Things will get better. Have you finished your homework?"

"Yes, Mom," I muttered. She just didn't get it. Sure, no one had been outright mean to me, but no one had been *nice* either. I wanted to tell her about the blockhead guy, but she had already moved on to a whole new subject.

"Oh, and, Tiphanie, this morning I saw all those clothes you scattered across your bed and on the floor. Just because we can afford to buy a few more things now doesn't mean you can treat your belongings with such carelessness. Please hang them up."

I sighed and left the kitchen. On the way to my bedroom I stopped in the living room to try Renee again.

"Hello?"

"Renee! Where have you been?" I asked. "I've been calling you all afternoon!"

"Girl, we were having too much fun at Brooks'. It was like *everyone* was hanging out there today!" Renee's voice was brimming with happiness. My homesickness returned with a vengeance.

"Oh, yeah?" I said, without much enthusiasm. "Who was there?"

"I'm telling you, everybody! Oh, you know that fine senior guy that we used to pass every day on the way to third period? He was there, and girl, he's a real cool cat."

I closed my eyes and pictured Renee and me bounding up the stairs to our social studies class, passing Mr. Fine Senior Guy and trying to sneak looks at him without him seeing.

"Oh, and the quarterback of the football team was there too," Renee continued. "I needed eleven more cents to get my stuff and he actually gave it to me! Girl, you should have been there. I got in trouble for coming home late, but it was worth it. So, what's your school like?"

Lonely. White. Did I mention lonely? I wanted to say. Instead I said, "It's fine. It's school. Not much different than Grove, I guess."

"See, it's not gonna be as bad as you thought," Renee said. "Oh, hey, Mo wanted me to say hi to you!"

That was about all I could take. I still had a major crush on Mo, and who knew when I'd get to see him again?

"Tell him 'What's up?' for me," I said quietly. "I better go. You know how the parents are about homework."

"Yeah, yeah, I know how they are. What was it your mom

always said to us? Oh, wait, I remember. 'Good better best, never let it rest, till your good gets better and your better gets best.' I gotta get going on my homework too, before my mom has a spaz attack. Talk to ya later!"

"Bye," I said.

As I hung up, I began to regret calling. It would have been less painful not to know what I was missing.

Tuesday was more of the same. In English I watched as everyone sat as far away from me as possible—everyone except the friendly-faced guy, who nodded at me. I was so surprised that I only nodded back. Then I spent the whole class wondering why I didn't say hi and ask what his name was.

Math was wonderful, again, and I had another successful visit to the chalkboard. But then in history we were discussing the Boston Massacre and the stupid textbook didn't even mention Crispus Attucks. I raised my hand.

"This textbook doesn't say anything about Crispus Attucks," I said. "You know, the first guy killed in the Revolutionary War." The teacher looked at me like I was crazy. "He was Black. I figured he'd be mentioned is all."

My teacher stared at me and said, "Yes, thank you for that bit of trivia, Tiphanie. Now moving on . . ."

I leaned back in my chair and tried not to roll my eyes at her.

Next was French class, and, well, that was the one class where I didn't mind not talking so much.

At lunch I grabbed some food, sat at my big table, and began doing my history homework. It helped keep my mind off the fact that I was eating alone again.

It was in science that the only interesting thing happened that day, and really it wasn't all that interesting, but I was getting a little desperate.

"Okay, class, first things first," Mr. Wells said. "As you know, our most important project will be the science fair held at the end of the semester. Now, last year I randomly assigned the class into groups." He held up his hand to quiet the moans and whines from my classmates. "This year, however, in an attempt to avoid personality conflicts, I'm allowing you to create your own groups. I'll need four groups of six."

The classroom erupted into cheers, but I groaned silently as I looked around the room, trying to figure out my options. To my left, the giggling blond girls from English had already grouped themselves together and were squealing with delight. Behind them was a random collection of students who seemed already to be a full group too. In the last seats in my row was another group of six—group number three. It looked like there were only four people not in a group yet, and all of them were boys. One of them was the friendly guy from English.

Mr. Wells came and stood next to my desk and addressed the group behind me. "Okay, what about you guys, what have you got?" he asked.

A blond guy answered, "Well, so far we have me, Todd, Andy, and Steve." Mr. Wells nodded and jotted down the names on his notepad. "Oh, and Bradley, he'll be in our group too."

"That's right," Mr. Wells said, consulting his list. "He's been out with strep throat. He should be back soon, I think. So that makes five. And with Tiphanie here you'll have six, okay?" He gave the guys a look as if to tell them, "Don't you dare say a word."

I glanced at the group. They looked back at me and shrugged. They didn't say a word.

4

Wednesday I returned to school without fear, but with a lot of loneliness. I was jostled in the hall and bumped into just like I would have been at my old school, but I was beginning to wonder if my classmates really were racist, or if possibly they were just rude. Like when I held the door open for a girl rushing to beat the bell for my math class. She hadn't bothered to thank me, hadn't even acknowledged I was standing there holding the door open for her. Was she a bigot or simply ill-mannered? I mean, I'd seen my classmates act plenty rude to each other in the past three days, and that didn't seem to have anything to do with skin color. I was starting to think that they didn't know how to react or talk to me any more than I knew how to deal with them.

I'd always been more of a talker than an observer, but at Brent Hills my personality seemed to flip. I watched the ears of the friendly-faced guy in English—Todd Lewan was his name—turn red when this girl passed him a note while the teacher's back was turned. I watched Blockhead—by then I knew his name was Clay Murphy, but I preferred to think of him as simply Blockhead, capital *B*—scowl every time he got a math problem wrong at the board. I watched this blond guy in French attempt to get a girl's attention, even though she was clearly into this curly-haired guy. And in home ec I watched the same few blond girls in class make snide remarks to the hippy girl who usually sat next to me. And all the time, while I was watching, I wished I could be a participant instead of a spectator.

At lunch on Friday, I was sitting alone at my table, listening to random snippets of conversations.

"Lori can't seriously be thinking that Dean is interested in her . . ."

"I can't believe Mrs. Anderson gave us that surprise test! How unfair . . ."

"Are you going to the rec center tomorrow night?"

"So is this the loser table or what?"

Wait! That last comment was actually directed at me! I stared up at the hippy girl from home ec. She was standing beside my chair, paper bag in hand, smirking at me. Unlike the rest of my classmates, she wasn't wearing a pair of hip-huggers or a miniskirt with a coordinating head scarf. She looked like someone I'd seen in pictures of Woodstock, with the same flowy skirt she'd been wearing the day before and her long blond hair parted straight down the middle.

"You aren't deaf, are you?" she said, tilting her head and looking at me closely. "I mean, I assumed you sat here by yourself every day because you're Black and therefore a loser. Not because you're like a deaf-mute or something. But then I don't recall having heard you verbalize a thing."

"Excuse me?" I said finally. I was wary. Not only was this girl the first person to have approached me at Brent Hills, but I'd seen her talking to Blockhead a little too often for me to trust her much.

"Ah, good, not a deaf-dumb-mute," she said with a grin. "Just slow on the uptake. I said, 'Is . . . this . . . the . . . loser . . . table?' "

I looked into her eyes, and surprisingly, I didn't see any meanness in there. I did see something I recognized, though—loneliness. "Well, if you sit here it will be," I told her. "Right now it's the Black girl table."

She laughed and promptly sat in the chair right next to me. "Hi," she said. "Jackie Sue Webster."

"Hi, I'm . . ."

"Yeah, I know who you are. How could anyone not? You're currently the talk of the school. It's Tiphanie, right? Spelled wrong."

"It's a name. How can it be spelled wrong? What do you mean I'm the talk of the school?"

"Trust me. Your name is spelled wrong. And hell, yeah, you're the talk of the school. The girls—well, about half of them—like the way you dress. But they think they have nothing in common with you because you're Black, so trying to make friends with you would be a waste of time. Then about a fourth of them despise the fact that you're here, since they think your presence soils their pristine way of life. They hope you'll fail each class miserably so they can feel superior to you like their parents tell them they are. And the final fourth are so screwed up with their own personal issues that they don't have any spare time to think about you one way or another. And as for the boys, well, one or two of them would love to ask you out, but will never do so because the other ninety-nine percent wouldn't let them live it down. Enjoying school so far?"

This all came as a surprise to me, since up to a few seconds ago no one had said a word to me. Literally, *no one* had said *a word* to me. It gave me a perverse thrill to learn that I wasn't really being ignored, just silently sized up.

"And you?" I asked. "Which group do you fall into?"

"Who, me? I'm an anomaly," Jackie Sue said proudly.

"Pardon me? A what?" I was shocked that this hippy girl knew a word I didn't. I mean, I knew you weren't supposed to judge a book by its cover, but still.

"*Anomaly.* A glitch, an incongruity and abnormality, if you will."

"Excuse me?"

"My, aren't we the polite one? I don't fit into any known category. I am a free spirit."

"Oh, really?"

"Why, yes. I'm from the other side of Sheridan Boulevard," she whispered conspiratorially.

"Ah, I see." That explained a lot.

Brent Hills High was located in a mid-to-upper-class neighborhood to the west of Sheridan Boulevard, the four-lane street that separated Brent Hills from the older part of town. Like the majority of my classmates, I lived on the west side of the street, in a clump of new houses nestled against the foothills in one of those brand-spanking-new developments where the houses all look eerily alike—the perfect American suburb. The neighborhood that Jackie Sue came from was littered with trailer parks, subsidized housing, and broken-down rental homes. Coming from a place like that, she might as well have been Black like me.

"I am walking talking trailer trash," Jackie Sue said grandly, as if announcing she was descended from Queen Elizabeth. "And as such I am free to do whatever I want. I'll never amount to anything anyway."

"So, as an anomaly, you can just plop right down and talk to the new scary Black girl, eh?" I asked.

"You're damn skippy I can. I don't have to worry about it getting around the country club that I've been rubbing elbows with the likes of you."

I grinned at her. "Yes, well, what if I told you I wasn't supposed to be conversing with a poor unfortunate like *you*? What if it gets around *my* father's club? How would *I* explain it?"

Jackie Sue laughed as she pulled her food out of her paper sack. She put an apple and a handful of grapes in front, a peanut butter and honey sandwich behind that, and last a Twinkie. After her food was lined up in a straight line she proceeded to eat the Twinkie.

"You are confused," she said between dainty bites of sponge cake. "It's common knowledge that *your* being with *me* is a step up for you, regardless of my being poor. Poor white is still white, you know. I'm a step up for you, but you're a step down for me. I don't mind, though—I'll forgive you." Jackie Sue finished off the Twinkie and started on her sandwich.

It was my turn to laugh. Such blatant honesty was refreshing. "You're wrong," I said. "Being poor *is* a step below Black, at least where I come from. It certainly would be at my dad's club. And why bother making a line for your food if you're going to start at the back anyway?" I asked.

"This isn't the back, it's the front," Jackie Sue answered in between bites. "What sort of club would let your father in? I assume he's Black too. Or are you adopted by rich white do-gooders or something?"

"My dad is Black, just like me. No, it's the back. The front is closest to you."

"I've never met a Black man before. Does he look like Harry Belafonte or Sidney Poitier? It's my food and I say this is the front."

"Even if it is the front, you're still eating backward by eating the Twinkie first. And my dad doesn't look like either of those guys. Who does your mom look like? Carol Brady or Mrs. Partridge?"

That comment made Jackie Sue guffaw so loudly the kids who were still trying to ignore me actually turned to look directly at us. For the first time in four and a half days I felt fully visible, which was a pretty nice feeling.

"So how's tomorrow at about twelve-thirty?" Jackie Sue asked once her laughter had subsided.

"Huh?"

"Very eloquent, Tip. Tomorrow. Me at your house at

twelve-thirty. To meet your father, of course. He'll be home, won't he?" she asked.

"Yes, he'll be home," I said, a little surprised at this sudden turn of events. "Okay, sure, that's fine. I live at 20—"

"I know where you live. Everyone does, you know."

No, I didn't know that. It was a little creepy.

"Okay," I said. "Then we'll cross Sheridan and I'll meet your mother . . . Mrs. Carol Brady."

Jackie Sue's smile faded. "She'll be at work. You'll have to wait. Seriously, though. Is there really a club only for Black people?"

"Yes, Jackie Sue," I answered, "there really is. The Eagles Club, but it's only for Black men. No women allowed. We Blacks like to discriminate too, you know."

Her eyebrows shot up and I chuckled. Did she really think Blacks were that different?

For the rest of the period we ate our lunch without talking. I would have thought that after a week of silence I'd want to gab up a storm, but for some reason, with Jackie Sue, the quiet was okay.

5

My father did not look like Harry Belafonte, or Sidney Poitier, or even Flip Wilson, much to the obvious disappointment of Jackie Sue. He was a caramel-colored man with a pencil-thin mustache, slightly wavy hair that was graying at the temples, and little round glasses. Essentially a bank nerd. After meeting him, Jackie Sue whispered into my ear, "He looks like some Black guy you'd see on the street." She sounded so let down.

"I thought you said you've never seen a Black guy," I whispered back with a laugh.

"No. I said I've never *met* a Black man. I've *seen* them before."

"So now what, are you going home?"

"Home? Perish the thought, my dear girl. I am here to delight you with my company."

"Lucky me."

We stood there for a moment, looking at each other, not knowing what to do with ourselves. I wondered how this friendship was going to last if we didn't know how to spend an afternoon together.

"How about some food?" Jackie Sue said, breaking the silence. "I can eat your food, right? I mean, it's not something weird?"

"Well, aside from the fried monkey brains, it's pretty normal stuff. Kitchen's this way."

We padded across the shag carpeting of the beautifully decorated and never used living room, and into the kitchen, where my mother was heating up leftovers for lunch.

"Hey, Mommy, this is Jackie Sue Webster, a girl from school. Jackie Sue, this is my mother, Mrs. Baker."

"Hello, Jackie Sue, it's a pleasure to meet you," my mother said. She sounded polite enough, but I could tell she was sizing Jackie Sue up. And from the way she held her mouth, it was obvious that Jackie Sue—dressed in worn, slightly dingy clothes, looking every bit as poor as she was—had come up lacking. Nevertheless, my mother extended her hand to her. Jackie Sue's eyebrow shot up at my mother's formality, but she shook her hand and then took a seat at our new kitchen table.

"You call her Mommy, huh?" Jackie Sue asked after my mother had left us in peace.

"Yep. Sure do."

"Well, isn't that the sweetest thing," Jackie Sue replied.

"What do you call your mother?"

"To her face or behind her back?"

I looked over at her in curiosity. "Either."

"To her face I call her Ma. Behind her back, well, let's say

35

that in this pristine environment I can't say it out loud for fear it will soil the atmosphere. Do I have to eat this spinach? I hate spinach."

" 'Pristine environment'? What's with you? And it's not spinach. Those are greens. Collard greens to be precise. Try them. One bite. It's the rule."

Jackie Sue stared at her plate for a moment, and then slowly took a tiny bite of greens. She shrugged after tasting them. "They're all right, I guess. Do I have to eat it all to get dessert? Is that a rule too?"

I smiled and shook my head. "Really though, what's with the fancy words?" I asked her. "I don't think I've ever met anybody my age who talks like you."

Jackie Sue shrugged and took another, slightly bigger, bite of greens. "Words are free. Since I can't have fancy new clothes, I might as well have elaborate new words." She paused as she concentrated on her food. "Are you going to eat that chicken?" she said at last.

Jackie Sue had finished her chicken. I was only half done with mine. I hadn't noticed how quickly she'd been eating.

"Yes, I plan to. Do you want seconds? There's plenty."

"Thanks, I'm starving. There wasn't much food around for breakfast this morning," she said.

I took her plate and added another piece of chicken and some bread.

"You can go ahead and add some greens and more sweet potatoes too," Jackie Sue said softly.

"So, are you the only 'free spirit' at school? Or are there others?" I asked, giving her generous servings of food.

Between bites, Jackie Sue gave me the complete rundown of the cliques and groups at school. She'd gone to school with most of our classmates since junior high, so she was full of opinions about them.

"Well, let's see. There are the girls who always sit near the front door in the lunchroom."

"You mean that group of blondes who giggle all the time?" I asked.

"Yeah, that's them. I call them the Barbies. They all have older sisters in twelfth grade so they think that makes them important, like school's some sort of oligarchy or something. But really, no one likes them all that much."

"Well, why aren't you a Barbie?" I asked. "You're blond." Jackie Sue wasn't Marcia Brady pretty, but she was attractive in her own way. Her face was a little on the horsey side, but except for the section that she gnawed on all the time, her hair was a full and shiny strawberry blond. And she had big beautiful bright green eyes that twinkled.

"Perish the thought," Jackie Sue said, waving the idea off. "Besides, poor supersedes blond. Anyway, let's see. There's the group of boys that sit way in the back of the cafeteria. They're the freshman jocks. All they care about is sports. They're like the kings of the freshman boys, in a survival-of-the-fittest, *Lord of the Flies* kind of way."

"Okay, go on," I said. Knowing all this made me feel like less of an outsider.

"Then there's the nerd squad. They're quite egalitarian. They actually have both boys *and* girls in their group. They are the smart ones, but they aren't pretty or cute enough to have much power. Then there's a whole bunch of people that hang with just one other person, or maybe two other people. Like Denise LaFay and Gretchen Turner, or Jimmy Cooper, Brian Bates, and Al Walls. Of course there's the spic group. They . . ." She stopped talking when she saw the look on my face. "What?" she asked.

"Well, if you use a word like that to describe the Mexican or Spanish kids," I snapped, "then what types of words do you use to describe me?"

Jackie Sue fumbled with her fork. I could tell she felt embarrassed, but I didn't care. If we were going to be friends— and I wanted to be friends with her—then we had to be upfront with each other.

"Okay," she said finally. "I comprehend. But how is me using *that* word different from me calling blond girls Barbies, or white boys nerds or jocks?"

I was quiet for a minute, trying to find the words to explain the difference.

"Well, if people want to stop being a Barbie or a geek, they can," I said at last. "They can dye their hair, get bad grades, or change who they hang with. But being Mexican or Spanish or Black isn't something you can change. It's what people are born being; not who they've decided to hang with or how they act. I don't know. Barbie, geek, it's more of a description, not a definition. I don't think it's right to use words like spic, or wop or whatever." I shrugged. "Those words are always said with hate, and I'd rather not hear them being used, if you don't mind." After a moment of silence I added, "Besides, with all your fancy words I would think that you could come up with some better ones." I picked up our now empty plates and carried them to the sink.

Finally Jackie Sue said, "Okay. Fair enough. Well then, all boys and girls of Mexican descent hang together." She looked at me for approval. I nodded, trying to determine whether I heard a tinge of sarcasm beneath her words. I decided to not look too hard. Sometimes if you were looking for racism you'd find it whether it was there or not. That's not how I wanted to spend my time with my new friend, constantly on the lookout for things to be insulted by.

"Lastly, and most importantly," Jackie Sue said, "there's the new group. The Oreo Squad, I call them. I think they'll run the school, or at least give everyone else a run for their money."

"Really?" I asked. "Who are they?"

"You and me, of course! Who else?"

6

Even though Jackie Sue and I only got to hang out during lunch, home ec, and the short time we had during passing periods, just knowing she was there made going to school the following week easier. Still, I felt a giant rush of relief when that Tuesday afternoon Bradley Jepperson came strolling into physical science. I was a bit hesitant to talk to him, though. I had no way of knowing how he'd react to me being there, and after seeing him receive a royal welcome from the guys behind me, I was even more skeptical. What if Bradley had actually liked being the only Black kid at Brent Hills High?

When he finally spotted me a look of surprise appeared on his face. He came up to my desk and grinned at me. "Are you real?" he said, gently poking me in the shoulder. "Please tell me you're real."

"I'm real," I said with a smile. "Although I'm pretty sure you're a figment of my imagination. I mean, they told me there were other Blacks out here in Brent Hills, but I was beginning to think they all lived in my house."

After class, Bradley offered to walk me to my locker. We were turning a corner when all of a sudden I saw Jackie Sue being dragged by the arm by no other than Blockhead.

"What is with that boy?" I asked Bradley. "He's the only person who goes out of his way to be rude to me."

Bradley looked around to see who I was talking about. "Oh, Clay?" he asked, rolling his eyes. "He's a redneck, from the trailer park. Don't pay him any attention."

Glancing over I saw that Blockhead had Jackie Sue backed up against a wall and was pointing at her as if he was a parent and she was a disobedient child. What was the deal with the two of them anyway? I wanted to go over and pull Jackie Sue away, but before I could make a move Bradley told me he wanted to introduce me to the Mexican kids, so I went with him. Besides, I hadn't known Jackie Sue long enough to get in her business like that. At least not yet.

On Wednesday Jackie Sue sat down next to me at the lunch table, and while arranging her food, launched into a report of what our classmates had been saying about me. Apparently everyone had been asking her questions about the new Black girl, not knowing she'd come straight to me with everything they said. Jackie Sue was eating up the new-found attention, and she got a kick out of acting like some undercover spy.

"The Barbies want to know where you shop at. They can't

figure out where you get your clothes and it's driving them nuts. I think they want to copy your fashion stylings."

I laughed. "I get most of my stuff at this place in Five Points. Tell them I'd be happy to give them directions." Five Points was the center of the Blackest neighborhood in Denver. I doubted they'd start shopping there.

"Yeah, I think that your unique haute couture will remain your own. Oh, and Celeste Henderson—you know that red-haired chick? She wants to know how you get your hair like that."

That day I was wearing my hair in two giant Afro puffs. I'd spent all of last year letting my relaxer grow out so I could wear an Afro like everyone else in my old neighborhood, much to my mother's dismay. Unfortunately, I hated the way I looked in one. I wasn't crazy about the Afro puff look either. Sometime soon I would have to put my pride aside and ask my mother to take me to the beauty shop to get a relaxer put in.

"Girl, she can't even do this," I told Jackie Sue, shaking my head. "This is a real live natural. I can't help her with that. What else?"

"Well, Jill, Gretchen, Cindy, and Vicki are wondering if you and Bradley are a couple now that you've met," Jackie Sue said with a smirk. "I was kind of curious about that as well."

"Bradley's cool," I answered. "But we're just friends. I don't see that changing anytime soon."

"Why not?" Jackie Sue asked between bites of peanut

butter and honey sandwich. "You guys have a lot in common."

"We do? Like what?"

Jackie Sue shrugged. "I don't know. I just assumed you did."

"Why would you assume that? Do you know him well enough to know what he likes? Do you know what his hobbies are? What he likes to do?" I knew what she was getting at, but I wasn't going to make it easy for her.

"Well, no, but, I figured, you know. You're both here, and, well, there's the Black thing."

"So you figure if there's a Black boy and a Black girl anywhere near each other they'll automatically start going out together? Are you saying I could point to any white dude in here and *bam!* you two would be a couple? It's that simple?"

Jackie Sue looked down and began chewing on her hair. "I'm sorry," she said. "I guess it is insulting to presume that you and Bradley would automatically be compatible due to your shared ancestry."

I sighed and let her off the hook. "Jeez, you and your words," I said. "Yes, professor, it is insulting to presume Bradley and I are automatically, um, oh, whatever. What else ya got?"

"Let's see, oh, yes. Todd Lewan thinks you smell nice. Like chocolate, he said." Jackie Sue laughed. "I told him that he was being unimaginative and obvious, and that you smelled like Ivory soap, like everyone else. I said your skin color was confusing his olfactory senses."

This report, more than any other, got my full attention. "You should have told him that what he smelled was Oreo cookies, but only when you and I are standing together and our scents intermingle," I said.

We laughed.

"Todd would never understand that," Jackie Sue said. "You know he's dense."

"I don't get the feeling he's dense," I said. "I think he just takes everything at face value. The real question is why does he smell me at all?"

Jackie Sue wiggled her eyebrows at me. "I think he might have a thing for chocolate," she said.

"Yeah, whatever," I said, but my stomach felt a little fluttery. "Hey, speaking of having a thing for someone, what's going on between you and Clay Murphy? Are you guys an item or something?"

"Me and Clay? Really, Tippy, I thought you knew me better than that. I will not be tied down by one boy."

"I saw you guys huddled in the corner yesterday talking," I said, frowning at her. "He hates me, I can tell. What could you possibly have been talking about?"

"We . . . I . . . he . . . we had to talk, that's all," Jackie Sue said. She looked away, which made me uneasy.

"About?"

"Just stuff," she said, still not meeting my eye. Then she shoved the last of her sandwich in her mouth and stood up. "The bell is about to ring. I'll see you after school."

She swept the trash from her lunch into her paper bag and quickly turned and walked out of the lunchroom a second before the bell actually rang. I sat there, stunned at her abrupt departure.

I thought about Jackie Sue and Clay for a minute, but then decided I'd rather think about Todd Lewan. I was surprised to hear that he was talking to Jackie Sue about how I smelled. And Jackie Sue was wrong. I didn't use Ivory. I used Ambi Soap, and because it had cocoa butter in it, it did actually smell like chocolate—well, cocoa, to be exact. There was something about Todd noticing such a personal detail about me that I appreciated. After days of feeling invisible, the fact that someone else was taking the time to smell me and analyze the scent made me happy. That took thought, and time, and sniffing.

7

The next day I went into English with a plan. When Todd sat down behind me, I turned around and smiled at him. He looked startled.

"Hi, Todd, do you happen to have an extra pencil?" I asked cheerfully, as if we spoke to each other every day. Of course, I had plenty of pencils—at least two right in the pencil bag on the desk in front of me.

Todd seemed stunned that I'd said something to him. While he stared at me in wide-eyed silence, I took a good look at him. He was fair-skinned, with a sprinkling of freckles across the bridge of his nose, dark brown eyes, and the kind of incredible eyelashes that girls would kill for—thick, long, and darn near perfect. He was kind of a fox, actually, for a white dude. Sort of like Chachi on *Happy Days*.

"Wow, you've got great eyelashes."

Oops, had I said that out loud? Todd's face turned bright pink. I sighed and turned around. It had been worth a try anyway.

Suddenly I felt a tap on my shoulder. I turned and saw Todd extending a pencil to me, his face still glowing red.

I grinned at him. "Thanks. Thanks a lot, Todd."

"You're welcome, Tiphanie."

Ahh, success.

During the next passing period, Jackie Sue and I were leaning against her locker as I told her about my brief, yet very meaningful, conversation with Todd, when Clay stepped right between us and started yapping at Jackie Sue.

"Clay!" she cried. "I was talking to Tiphanie. Can't you wait?"

Clay gave me a dismissive wave of his hand. "Not for *her*. I don't know why you spend so much time with her anyway." He said this as if I couldn't hear every word he was saying. "She should move back to the ghetto with the rest of them."

"Excuse me?" Jackie Sue and I said in unison.

"You need to spend less time with her, Jackie Sue," Clay said. "Your rep isn't all that great to begin with. Hanging out with the token Black chick isn't going to help much."

"Clay, you aren't my boss," Jackie Sue said, but it sounded halfhearted. "You can't tell me what to do."

"Yeah, well, maybe I should just mention this little friendship of yours to my dad," Clay said. "Especially around the first of the month." Then he turned and spoke to me directly for the first time ever. "This isn't even your country," he sneered. "Why don't you go back to the motherland?"

"Are you out of your mind?" I said. I looked over at

Jackie Sue to see if she had a few choice college words to put Clay in his place, but she had started chewing on her hair instead.

"You people are nothing but a drain on this country," Clay said.

That was it.

"You're an idiot," I told him. "Clearly, you don't know anything about history. Not only am I willing to bet that *my* ancestors have been here much longer than yours, but I bet *yours* came over because whatever country they came from kicked them out." From the corner of my eye I could see people looking over at us, slowing down to watch, but I didn't care. "*My* people built this country with our hands and our backs. For free!" Suddenly I was sounding like my parents, only louder.

Jackie Sue whispered, "Shhh!" and started pulling on my arm. "Just let it go, Tiphanie! Come on! Bell's about to ring."

I turned and looked at her with surprise. She was supposed to be my friend. Why wasn't she standing up for me?

"You know, I'm glad that man shot Lincoln," Clay continued. "My dad says he ruined this country with all that 'free the slaves' crap!"

"You have got to be kidding me!" I shouted. "You must be some special kind of crazy to think that—"

Suddenly, Mrs. Steele, a math teacher from the class across the hall, came barreling out of her room. On a good day she looked mean, with her cold gray eyes and her stiff gray hair and her ever-present frown, but that day she looked downright evil.

"What is going on here?" she said, looking from Clay to Jackie Sue to me.

Before I could say a word, Clay started in, "I really don't know, Mrs. Steele. She just started hollering and screaming at me for no reason. I didn't do anything to her."

Mrs. Steele turned to Jackie Sue. "Is this true?" she asked.

"Well, yes. I guess," Jackie Sue mumbled, looking down at her feet.

My mouth dropped open.

"You!" Mrs. Steele said, pointing at me. "Straight to the office, this instant! Don't stand there looking so surprised. Screaming and shouting is not allowed at this school."

"What about Clay?" I asked. "He started it."

"It was your screaming and shouting I heard," Mrs. Steele said. "No one else's."

Behind Mrs. Steele's back, Clay was smirking.

"March! You two, off to class."

As Jackie Sue turned to go, she silently mouthed "Sorry!" But that wouldn't even cut it. I headed toward the office.

When I got to the office I told Miss Tingle I'd been sent by Mrs. Steele. Tsking with disapproval, she knocked on the principal's office and announced to Mr. Daniels that I was there for disciplinary matters.

The word *disciplinary* jolted me out of my anger. Disciplinary meant a call to my parents. If I got in trouble at school, especially when I was supposed to be representing my race, I would never be allowed out again.

"Good morning, Tiphanie," Mr. Daniels said when I walked into his office. He clasped my hand into his two big, warm palms. "Before we talk about what brings you here, first, I must apologize to you."

"Huh?" I said. "I beg your pardon?"

He chuckled. "Well, I usually like to pull in the new students after their first week to make sure they're okay. Just to assure myself that they're finding their way around, not having problems in class or with their schoolmates. And in your case, especially with you being one of two Afro-Americans here, it was really quite neglectful of me not to have called you in right away. As I'm sure you've found, most of the students here in Brent Hills haven't had much exposure to people of other ethnicities. I hope they aren't being cruel to you."

"Well," I said, "they haven't fallen all over themselves to welcome me, but for the most part they've been cool. I've only had a problem with one person so far."

"Good, good," Mr. Daniels said. He appeared to be genuinely relieved to hear that. "So what brings you here?"

"Um, well, you know that one person I mentioned? We got into a bit of a . . . uh . . ." I cast around in my head for a Jackie Sue–like word. "A verbal disagreement that was a bit too loud for Mrs. Steele. So she sent *me* here and let *Clay* go back to class."

Mr. Daniels nodded. "Ah, yes, Mrs. Steele. And let me guess, Clay Murphy. I see. Well, I suggest that next time you talk with Mr. Murphy, you keep your voice down. You should also keep in mind that sometimes people are incapable of hearing what you have to say no matter how loudly you say it." He stood up. "All righty then, back to class you go. If you have any other problems, feel free to come by. Oh, and I'd sure like it if you'd say hi to me in the hallways. Kids never say hi to me in the hallways."

I sat there for a minute, staring at him. *Keep your voice down?* That was it?

"Okay, sir," I said, rising to my feet. "I'll do that."

"Good! Now go on. Miss Tingle will give you a pass for class. Study hard! Learn something new today!"

I got a pass and headed for class with a tiny smile on my face that lasted for a whole three periods, until I walked into the cafeteria and saw Jackie Sue.

I was still angry with her. Why hadn't she had my back earlier? When she approached our table I turned away from her. She sat beside me anyway.

"Hi," she said quietly. "Did you get into an imbroglio?"

"What?" I snapped, still not looking at her.

"Trouble," she said softly. "Did you get into trouble?"

"No, I didn't. Not once I explained *my* side to the principal. Something you didn't bother to do to Mrs. Steele."

"I'm sorry," she said.

"I can't believe you did that to me, Jackie Sue," I said, turning to look at her. "You heard what Clay said. It was plain racist, and you stood there as if what he was saying was okay."

Jackie Sue nodded without saying anything.

"I don't get it," I continued. "I mean, were you trying to impress him or something? He's not your boyfriend, is he?"

She didn't say anything, only glanced over at the table where Clay and his friend were sitting. I could tell they were talking about what had happened because they were looking over at us—at me—and laughing. Jackie Sue looked miserable.

I didn't get what was going on, or why Jackie Sue wouldn't tell me what the deal was with Clay. Part of me wanted to tell her to go away and leave me alone. But then I would have had to go back to being by myself again, lonely and friendless, and I didn't want that. So I decided that I'd forgive her. I'd be the friend to her that I wanted her to be to me. Do unto others, right?

Well, at least this time.

8

When Clay appeared at Jackie Sue's locker after school that afternoon, I moved to the side and crossed my arms with an attitude, giving him the evilest look I could muster. But I bit my tongue, gritted my teeth, and said nothing. Based on how Clay went out of his way to talk to her, it was becoming clear to me that he definitely had a thing for Jackie Sue. What, if anything, she saw in him was totally beyond my comprehension.

"Why don't you go out with Todd, instead of that wannabe Herman Munster?" I asked Jackie Sue while we were walking home that day. "He's far better-looking than Clay."

"First of all, I'm not going out with Clay or anyone else. Second of all, I've noticed that in about every conversation we've had lately, you bring up Todd. What is that all about?"

"Nothing," I mumbled. I wasn't ready to tell Jackie Sue I

might have a thing for Todd. Not as long as she was keeping secrets from me.

"Yeah, right," she said. "Come on, spill it."

"It's just that, besides you and Bradley, he's the only one at school I talk to."

"Liar. Today I saw you talking with Maria Villa and Teresa Garcia."

That was true. Ever since Bradley had introduced us, the Mexican kids had started chatting with me. I liked them, but didn't think any deep friendships would come of it. They had a way of talking to each other that kept me at arm's length. Every few words they would throw in some Spanish, so I could never quite follow their conversations.

"Well, yeah," I said. "That's true, but—"

"But what?" Jackie Sue cut in. "Get over your 'poor me' act. That pity party of yours is getting old. 'Poor little me! I'm the only Black girl in school. No one likes me, everybody hates me, blah, blah, blah.' Open your eyes, will you? Besides, being ignored by some of those snots is hardly the worst thing in life. There are people who have far worse things than that to deal with, you know."

I opened my mouth to disagree, but then I suddenly realized she might be right. "Okay, fine, Jackie Sue," I said with a pout. "But you don't have to yell at me."

"Quit pouting, Tip. It's unbecoming."

We walked the entire block in silence. When we got to the corner where we normally turned to go to my house, Jackie Sue walked to the light instead, as if she was going to cross Sheridan and head home.

"Hey, aren't you coming over?" I asked.

"No," Jackie Sue snapped. But after seeing the look on my face, her tone softened. "I gotta check on my mom."

"Are you sure you have a mom?" I said. "As far as I know you could've been hatched."

She gave me a reluctant grin. "Ha, ha, ha. You're very amusing."

"Hey, how about we go over to your house this afternoon?" I said. "I'd love to meet her!" I felt rude inviting myself over, but I figured we were good enough friends that Jackie Sue would overlook it.

"Um, you know, today's probably not a great day," she said, looking away from me. "My mom is . . . sick."

We stood there quietly for a moment. I was embarrassed I'd asked.

"Oh, well then, I hope she feels better soon," I muttered.

"Yeah, me too. Anyway, I gotta go."

As I stood waiting for the light to change, I wondered whether Jackie Sue's mother was really sick, or if she was keeping me from meeting her on purpose.

On Friday, not only did I have a nice little chat in English with Todd about how boring *The Odyssey* was, but in history, Denise LaFay and I laughed about last night's *Barney Miller* episode. And in French class, Troy Weingard and I practiced our recitation together. We both stunk, but it was fun anyway. It seemed like Jackie Sue had been right about me after all. I did have more friends than I'd realized.

By eighth period, I was in a great mood—until I walked

into the home economics room in time to hear Jill Wrightman saying, "You must really love that denim maxi-skirt, Jackie Sue. I mean, you're in it almost every single day. I'm surprised you aren't sick of wearing it, because I sure am sick of seeing it."

Jill's blond friends tittered. Jackie Sue's whole body tensed.

"Don't even answer, Jackie Sue," I said, pulling her toward our assigned sewing machines. Then I added loudly for everyone in the room to hear, "Jill's just jealous because they don't make cute skirts like yours nearly maxi enough to fit her wide behind. Even a size sixteen maxi on her would look like a mini."

I knew my parents would be furious if they found out I hadn't "kept a civil tongue in my mouth," but seeing the look on Jackie Sue's face—not to mention the look on Jill's—was worth it. Besides, my parents were the ones who had told me that injustice anywhere was a threat to justice everywhere. And in my world, a filthy-rich Jill picking on a dirt-poor Jackie Sue was definitely an injustice.

After dinner, my parents and I were settling into our Friday night routine—pulling out the air popcorn popper and crowding onto our couch to watch *M*A*S*H* and the *ABC Friday Night Movie*—when the phone rang. I went to answer it.

"Hi, Tiphanie?" a voice said. I had no idea who it was.

"Yes?"

"Um, hi," the voice said again. "It's Todd. Todd Lewan. From school?"

"Oh! Hi!" I answered. My stomach gave a lurch.

"Um, I got your number from Jackie Sue," he said. "I hope you don't mind."

"Oh, no problem," I answered.

Silence.

"So," he mumbled finally. "I was wondering if you had the science homework. The, um, page numbers and review questions numbers, and stuff."

"Sure," I said, vaguely wondering why he had gone through the trouble to get my number from Jackie Sue when he could have easily gotten the homework from any one of his guy friends. Then in a rush of excitement, I realized why. He'd called to talk to me! After giving him the homework information I racked my brain for something else to say, but nothing came to mind, especially with my parents sitting right there. Pretending I needed something from a different room, I carried the phone as far as the cord would stretch. I shut myself in the hall closet to ensure my privacy, shoving the extra towels out of the way, and I sat down to get comfortable.

"So, what are you doing tonight?" I asked him.

"Nothing," he answered. "What about you?"

"Just watching TV with my parents."

There was a long pause.

"Well, so, do you ski?" he asked.

"Nope," I said. Another moment of silence. I hurried to improvise. "I'd like to learn, though. Do you?"

"Yes! As much as possible! Only a few more days until Loveland opens up. It's always a big competition to see which resort opens first. Usually it's Loveland, sometimes A-Basin. Last year Loveland opened up October tenth! Right now they don't have much of a base, but they'll start running the lifts soon."

"Oh, so, you're big into skiing, huh?" I said.

"It's my favorite thing. I'd be happy to teach you." Todd sounded thrilled. "You should join the ski club at school. Once ski season starts we go up almost every weekend."

Todd then launched into a very—what was a good Jackie Sue word?—*tedious* conversation about skiing. I had no idea what he was talking about.

I felt a tug on the phone cord and poked my head out of the closet. My mother was looking down at me as if I'd lost my mind.

"Well, um, I gotta go," I mumbled to Todd. "The movie's about to start."

"Oh, okay, sure," he said. "I really like talking to you, Tiphanie. I'll see you at school on Monday. Bye."

"Yeah, later," I said. I hung up the phone and scrambled to my feet.

"What was so secretive that you had to sit in the linen closet to talk about?" my mother asked.

"Oh, you know," I muttered. "I just didn't want to disturb you guys."

"Uh-huh," she said. I scooted around her and tried to make a run for it. "So who was it? Renee?"

"Um, no," I said. "Someone from school."

"Oh!" she exclaimed. "Well, honey, that's great. I knew

it'd only be a matter of time before they all warmed up to you."

My mother smiled at me and squeezed my shoulder as we walked back to the couch. I didn't even roll my eyes— because maybe, just maybe, she was right.

9

Even though my mother insisted on waking me up at the crack of dawn Saturday morning for my all-day youth services project at church, I wasn't upset. It felt like a lifetime since I'd been back in my old neighborhood, especially since we hadn't gone to church last week.

Our church was one of the oldest African Methodist Episcopal churches in Denver—"old" being the most important part of the description. There were only a dozen or so young people in our congregation, so as a result, I was president of the youth group, co-president of the youth ushers, and secretary of the coming-of-age program. All those fancy titles really ended up meaning squat though, because the old people were so bossy that they always did everything themselves anyway.

When my mother dropped me off in front of the church, Simon hurried over to me with his arms outstretched, as if I would really give him a hug.

"Oh, look who came down from her suburb to grace us

with her presence," he said. "I still can't believe you left us like that." Simon had a major crush on me, and he was a spaz. His twin sister, Simone, was a wack job too. Luckily my friends Regina and Joseph were right behind him.

"Hey, Gina, what's going on?" I asked, turning my back to Simon.

"That view's fine with me too!" he said.

Gross.

"Well," Regina said wearily, "Mrs. Kelley said we needed to start setting up, but then she discovered she'd forgotten to buy the decorations. So now we're sitting here waiting because Mrs. Kelley had to drive to the store. Then, when Mrs. Taylor tried to open the Fellowship Hall so we could at least set up the tables, she discovered that it was still locked. So she had to go home and call a trustee to open it up."

The event we were having was a Back to School fair. Our church sat in the poorest part of Denver, so we'd invited the students from the surrounding neighborhood to come. We were going to set up a carnival with little games, and the prizes would be supplies and books that the church members had donated.

"So, Tip," said Regina, taking a seat on the lawn in front of the church. "What's your new school like?"

Joseph and I joined her on the grass, while Simon and Simone pulled out some yarn and began to play cat's cradle. Jeez, what were they, ten years old?

"Yeah," said Joseph. "How's the 'burbs? You guys been threatened by the Klan yet?"

Joseph was extremely distrustful of white people. He and

his mother had moved to Colorado a couple of years ago from Tupelo, Mississippi, after his father died under very suspicious circumstances. Joseph saw racism in everything.

"Um, no," I said.

"But you've been called out of your name, haven't you?" Joseph said. "Don't try to cover up for those racist pigs, Tip!"

"Joseph," I said. "Calm down. I'm still getting used to it out there. I mean, I am the only Black girl. But it hasn't really been all that—"

"Whoa!" Regina interrupted. "You mean you're the only one in the whole school? Dang. Your parents really jacked you up, didn't they?"

"Look, you run into any trouble, you let me know," Joseph said. "I can get together some of my friends, they're real close to the Panthers." Joseph was always claiming to know Black Panthers in Denver. I doubted that Denver had any, but then you never really knew.

Joseph saw the Black Panthers as heroes—the group that gave free lunches to children, patrolled streets to make them safer, and who were unfairly harassed by the government and hounded by J. Edgar Hoover. But many older Afro-Americans, like my parents, considered the Panthers a group of young, angry, militant Black hoodlums who were always involved in some sort of violent incident. They viewed them with a heavy dose of suspicion and a liberal sprinkling of fear—worrying that the Panthers would cancel out the civil rights progress that had been made in the past decade. As for me, well, I figured they must be a little good and a little bad, just like everyone else.

"We can caravan out to the 'burbs if you need us," Joseph continued. "Make sure they know this ain't no 1955."

I nodded, trying to visualize Joseph and his friends with their huge black Afros and dark sunglasses, marching up the street toward our new house. "Um, thanks, Joe."

"Anyway, don't forget where you come from, Tip," Joseph said. "Don't turn your back on your people. Because you know that's where Uncle Toms and Oreos come from, right? From hanging around too many white people."

Luckily, Mrs. Taylor and Mrs. Kelley arrived then so we could finally get to work. I was glad that the conversation had to come to an end. Even though I'd only been at Brent Hills High for a grand total of ten days, I was beginning to feel at home there. Did that mean I was a sellout?

That talk with Joseph haunted me all day Saturday and through the beginning of the next week. Did my looking forward to chatting with Todd before English class mean I was slowly becoming an Uncle Tom? Did my laughing at Denise's joke in social studies mean I was an Oreo—Black on the outside, white on the inside? And did the fact that I was still friends with Jackie Sue, even though she hadn't stood up to Clay for me, mean I wasn't fighting for my people? Had I begun to change and didn't even know it?

Tuesday after gym, I arrived at my physical science classroom to find a note on the door saying we'd be meeting in the library to start work on our science projects. I wandered into the library and looked around.

"Hey, Tip, over here!" a voice called out to me.

I turned and saw Bradley waving me toward a table that was filled with the rest of the boys in my group.

"Thanks, Bradley," I said, sitting down.

Bradley read off a sheet of mimeographed paper. "Okay, the first thing we're supposed to do is introduce ourselves. That's stupid. I mean, we've all known each other for years, right? Oh, wait. Tip, do you know everybody's name?"

"Well, yeah," I said, looking around at the table. I pointed to blond, blue-eyed Troy who sat at the far end of the table. "That's Troy Weingard. He's the one that all the Barbies are in love with."

The boys hooted and Troy looked at me with a sappy smile.

I pointed at the redhead next to him. "That's Steve Goddard. The girls think he's funny so he's on their top ten list of hot guys." Steve grinned with pleasure. I was on a roll.

"That's Andy Ryan," I said next, pointing to a boy who I disliked because he was so obnoxious. I paused, trying to think of something to say about him without having to tell the ugly truth. "He likes to annoy our teachers. That's—"

"Hey, what do the girls say about me?" Andy demanded.

I smiled with mock sympathy. "Sorry, Andy," I said with a shrug, which led to more hoots and shouts of laughter from the other guys. Andy flipped me off—like it was my fault every girl thought he was an idiot. "Hey, Andy, it's not my fault," I said sweetly. "See, it's little things like what you just did that kill ya. Girls really hate stuff like that, and you do *a lot* of stuff like that. Now, may I continue please?"

"Yes," all the other boys said in unison. It was becoming clear to me that my wealth of inside information regarding the boys' status among the girls at school was pretty valuable. I'd been the fly on the wall long enough to have heard everyone, except myself, spoken about, discussed, critiqued, and evaluated by my classmates—especially by the girls.

"That's Todd," I said, pointing. "I think, I mean, um, girls think he's foxy, but really, really quiet." Todd turned a deep red as he was buffeted about by playful shoving from his friends.

"Then last, but not least, there's you, Mr. Bradley Jepperson," I said, grinning at him. "All the girls think you're cool in a forbidden, superfly sort of way. The bold white girls love flirting with you, but they know they'd never be allowed to date you, even though they'd love to."

Bradley whooped. "Girl, you know you got that right!" he said, giving me a high five.

I sat back, feeling at ease. When I glanced over at the Barbies' table, they seemed to be much more interested in my science group than they were in the actual assignment.

The next day I was looking forward to science class almost as much as math class. During the time we spent working on our project, I learned quite a few things about boys in general, and that group of boys in particular. Bradley was indeed their leader—the others followed him without hesitation. He had a unique way of walking in their world while still being grounded in ours. It was a skill I hoped to learn.

The word about my unique position in science spread pretty quickly. And although I hadn't bothered to mention it to Jackie Sue, when we were walking home that afternoon she brought it up.

"Well, I guess you've finally found your special niche," she said.

"My what?" I asked. I disliked being reminded of her verbal superiority. It was much harder to show off one's math skills, which I found irritating.

"*Niche*. It means a situation specially suited to one's abilities . . . or a hole or crevice."

I sighed. "What are you talking about, Jackie Sue?"

"Don't get all cranky," she said. "I'm talking about your little science group."

"I'm not cranky, two-year-olds who miss their naps are cranky," I answered crankily. "So, you've heard about that, huh?"

"Of course I've heard about it," Jackie Sue replied. "It's like *the* topic of conversation."

"Is it really?" I asked.

"Yes, really, you egomaniacal goofball," she said. "Spill it."

"Well, what sort of information are you looking for?" I asked.

"What do they talk about? *Who* do they talk about?"

"Let's see," I said. "Well, they talk about three things and three things only: girls, sports, and farting. Not necessarily in that order."

"Farting?" she asked. "Passing gas is a topic of conversation?"

"Yes, unfortunately," I said. "Boys are really gross. You don't want to know any more details than that."

"Well, actually I kind of do," she said, grinning.

"Okay, but don't say I didn't warn you. See, they've taken the world of farts and categorized them into different types. There is the machine gun fart where it . . ."

"Oh, stop, stop, stop!" Jackie Sue looked utterly disgusted. "Tell me about the girl discussions."

"Well, Troy has a thing for Denise LaFay," I said.

"Really! I would have thought a Barbie would be more his speed."

"Yeah, me too," I said. "Of course, she does have those big . . . well she's more filled out than most of us. Anyway, you know Denise has been going out with Jon Stein for forever. It makes Troy crazy, 'cause Jon is shorter than he is."

"Jon's shorter than *Denise* is," Jackie Sue said.

As we continued walking, I told Jackie Sue all the little insights and secrets I'd gleaned from my new social group. But suddenly I noticed that Jackie Sue had gone quiet. I stopped my gossiping and looked at her.

"What's the matter, Jackie Sue?" I asked.

She smiled a cheerless little smile at me. "Nothing, it's just that . . ." She fell silent. We stopped at the corner where we parted ways on the rare day that Jackie Sue wasn't coming home with me. She was kicking at the autumn leaves, looking sad and melancholy.

"Jackie Sue?" I said quietly.

She looked up at me and I could see that she had tears in her eyes.

"Whoa. What's the matter?" I asked. I had seen her angry before, but crying? Never crying.

"I wish I had a different life," she said in a whisper.

I didn't know what to say to that. A defeated Jackie Sue was a Jackie Sue I didn't know how to deal with.

She rummaged through her ratty purse and pulled out a crumpled tissue. Then she walked to the crosswalk and pushed the button on the light.

"You're not coming over?" I asked.

"Not today," she said, blowing her nose.

"My mom made fried chicken last night. We have left-overs," I told her.

"Ohh, wish I could," she said with a sigh. "But I have things to do today." The light changed and the walk sign flashed at us. "See ya tomorrow," she said as she began to cross the street.

I stood there for a moment, watching Jackie Sue walk down the block toward the trailer park. What was going on with her?

"You lost or something?" I heard someone say.

I turned to find Clay sneering at me. Grant, his block-headed sidekick, was with him.

"No, Clay. I'm going home," I answered, even though it wasn't any of his business what I was doing.

"Back to Africa, is it then?" Clay said. Grant busted up laughing.

I glared at him and started walking home.

"Don't walk away mad, Tipha-pickanniny!" Clay shouted after me.

"Just walk away!" Grant added.

I could hear their laughter as I walked down the street, and I thought to myself, if I had to deal with Clay as much as Jackie Sue did, I'd wish for a different life too.

10

Troy was having a Halloween party. It had replaced, for the time being, the fart discussions during science. Thank goodness.

"So are we supposed to dress up for this shindig?" Bradley asked. He was carefully duct-taping Hot Wheels tracks together. We'd decided that for our group project we'd make a model roller coaster to demonstrate the effects of velocity.

"Yeah," Troy said with a shrug. "My mom is trying to talk me into having a costume contest. Like we're little kids or something."

"Does that mean we'll also be bobbing for apples?" Steve asked with a laugh. "Playing pin the tail on the donkey?"

"Or musical chairs," I added. "That's always a fun game."

"Et tu, Tiphanie?" Troy said.

"*Mais oui, mon ami,*" I answered with a grin. "*Je vais à la plage.*"

Troy chuckled and shook his head. "Man, your French is worse than mine."

"What are you coming as, Tippy?" Todd asked.

"Who, me?" I said, stunned. I'd assumed I wasn't invited. I looked over at Troy.

"Next Friday," he said. "Come in costume."

"Yeah, you gotta come, Tip," Steve said.

"Well, sure," I stammered. "I mean, if it's okay with your parents and all."

"Actually," Troy said, "my dad asked if I knew who you were last week. I guess your dad just approved this big loan for my dad's new construction project. I was like, 'Yeah, Dad, she's the only Black chick in our school. It's not like she's hard to spot.' He can be such a dork."

"Well, sure," I said. "I'll be there. Can I bring Jackie Sue? You know her, right?"

"Yeah, she can come," Troy answered. "I invited her boyfriend too, so I thought she'd be there anyway."

"Her boyfriend?" I asked. "Jackie Sue doesn't have a boyfriend."

"Yeah, she does," Steve said. "Clay."

"Clay Murphy isn't her boyfriend," I said. "What makes you think that?"

"Well, to hear him talk in gym they're hot and heavy," Andy said, giving Steve a nudge. "So if they aren't going steady, she's just easy."

"Shut up, Andy," I said.

Troy shrugged. "Anyway, she's welcome to come with you or with Clay. Hey, Todd, let's go as Starsky and Hutch."

As the conversation turned away from Jackie Sue and Clay, I began to wonder what Clay had been saying about Jackie Sue, and whether or not she knew about it. And most importantly, whether it was true.

On the walk home that day, I tried to bring up Clay again, but Jackie Sue changed the subject immediately. "So, are you just spending tomorrow night with your friend in Parkside?" she asked me. "Or is it the whole long weekend?"

The way she asked made me look over at her. She was chewing on her hair and looking straight ahead.

"Well, the whole thing," I answered slowly. We had fall break coming up, and my parents had agreed to let me spend the long weekend with Renee. But Jackie Sue looked so sad about it that I felt a pang of guilt.

When we reached my house, Jackie Sue and I immediately went into the kitchen. I set out our snack and tried to figure out a way to broach the subject of Clay again and what was going on between them, but I couldn't figure out what to say, or how to ask. So instead, we ate our snack, did our homework, and watched reruns of *Gilligan's Island* like we always did—just as if her life was as normal as mine.

Packing for my weekend at Renee's after Jackie Sue went home, I felt a weird blend of nervousness and excitement— like it was my first time staying at Renee's house instead of my hundredth. The plan was for my parents to drop me off at Renee's that evening and pick me up Sunday morning on the way to church.

Much to my relief, things seemed normal when I got there. Renee and I talked about all our old adventures and stayed up too late, laughing about stuff that happened in junior high. The next morning we watched Renee's brothers while her mom cooked breakfast. The boys ran wild in the yard, and Renee and I sat on the porch drinking orange juice, surveying the neighborhood.

"Oh, you should have been at school on Wednesday!" Renee said to me as we settled down on the porch swing. "Melinda was caught passing a note to Leo and Mrs. Roberts read it out loud! And then she corrected Melinda's grammar in front of the whole class! Mrs. Roberts sho 'nuff is cold-blooded."

I laughed. We'd both had a mutual dislike for Melinda ever since she embarrassed Renee about having torn-up shoes way back in the second grade. "Now which one is Leo again?" I asked. That was one of the new names that had crept into our conversations since I'd moved. It was getting harder and harder to keep the new people straight in my head.

"Leo and his family moved into the Graysons' old house right after you guys left," Renee explained. "He's kinda fine, but not so bright. Actually, he and Melinda would make a cute couple. Together they might have a full brain."

"So where's Mo?" I asked. Mo—Maurice Hall—was my first crush and kiss, and I'd been hoping to see him this weekend.

"Oh, girl, I forgot to tell you! He moved away. Out of the blue, his momma decided to go back to Georgia." Renee picked up an old shoe that was lying on the porch and threw it at her brothers, which was her way of making them stop throwing crab apples at passing cars. "One day he's walking home with us from school, the next thing we know, he and his momma are pulling away in a moving truck."

"Oh man," I said.

"Yeah, too bad, so sad. Anyway, the family that moved in have two boys. Twins. They're seniors, and *so* fine."

I nodded absentmindedly.

"So, are there any fine boys in that fancy neighborhood of yours?" she asked.

I immediately thought of Todd, but I knew he wasn't the kind of boy Renee was talking about. "Well, not really, I mean, there's just one Black guy, Bradley."

"Dang, that's right, you told me. I hope he's cute."

I wrinkled my nose. "He's okay. I mean, he's nice and all. I like him. I just don't like him, like him. He doesn't float my boat, you know?"

"Yeah, well, you better start *trying* to float, 'cause otherwise you're not going to have a boyfriend for years. I mean, only one Black dude?" Renee shook her head in disbelief. "That is so wrong."

"Well, there is this white boy named Todd," I said, watching Renee's brothers wrestling one another.

"A white boy?" she said. "So what?"

"Well, he's, you know, kinda cute." I looked over at her face and immediately regretted saying anything.

"Cute? Oh, uh-huh," she said.

"I'm not saying we're boyfriend-girlfriend or anything," I told her. "We've only talked on the phone once."

Renee was looking at me as if I had four eyes or something.

"What?" I said. But I knew. I knew what was coming.

"Yvonne and them were saying you'd be all whitewashed and stuff and I go, 'No.' And they went, 'Yeah, well, she's going to be living with all them white people and her father's all rich and stuff now. Plus, she always did talk kinda white even before she left.' And then I go, 'You guys are tripping. Tiphanie Jayne Baker is our home slice. She'll be back all the time, rocking her 'fro, hanging like she use to.' But now, I don't know. And your Afro *is* on its way out."

Then, without saying another word, Renee jumped off the porch and went down to the yard to yell at her little brothers, leaving me alone to think about what she'd said.

I didn't feel like a different person. My old friends had always teased me about the way I talked, too proper. But they didn't live with Morris and Annie Baker. Slang and bad grammar would never have flown in my house. Besides, I thought, I still liked the same food and the same music. I still dressed the same. But maybe I had changed and didn't even know it. So where did I belong? Here in Parkside? Or back in Brent Hills? Nowhere, that's where. The truth was, I didn't fit perfectly anywhere anymore.

For the rest of the weekend I went out of my way to be the old me, and act exactly like I used to when I lived around the block. On Saturday, Renee and I took the bus to the new mall with our old friends Sandra and Eva. We ran to the back of the bus, joking and talking loudly.

"Oh, she knows she shouldn't have worn that outside her house," I called out, pointing to a lady out the window. My friends laughed.

The four of us wandered through the mall, going from store to store, window-shopping. For the first time I actually had enough money in my purse to buy the few things that caught my eye, but I didn't spend a dime. I knew that would call attention to the fact that I wasn't exactly like my old friends anymore.

I was packed and ready to go when my parents arrived to pick me up for church on Sunday morning. They seemed surprised. A month ago, I would have dragged my feet and whined when it was time for a sleepover at Renee's to end, but this time I was anxious to leave.

I had thought I was going to be able to slide back into my place in the old neighborhood so easily, but it turned out I didn't fit there anymore. I was suddenly a puzzle piece without a puzzle to fit into.

11

When I got back home on Sunday afternoon, the first thing I wanted to do was hang out with Jackie Sue. When I called to invite her over she sounded as happy as I felt.

On the spur of the moment I decided to meet Jackie Sue halfway and walk with her to my house. After changing out of my church clothes, I walked toward our corner, and after a few minutes of waiting for her to appear I crossed the street and headed to her trailer park, figuring I'd meet her before I got all the way there. But before I knew it I was standing at the entrance to the park, trying to figure out which trailer was Jackie Sue's. That was when I saw Clay standing outside a trailer with a sign that read MANAGER/OWNER on the side.

He stomped over to me. "We don't allow your kind in here," he said.

"I have the right to go wherever I want to," I snapped. "Just ask the NAACP."

"You mean the National Association of Apes, Coons, and Possums?" he sneered. "They can't do anything. This is private property. You better leave." He took a step toward me and gave me a push.

"Get your hands off me!" I yelled, swinging my purse at him. It popped him squarely on the side of his big ole blockhead, and his face turned purple with anger, even though the only thing in my purse was a couple of dollars, my school ID, and some balled-up tissue.

"Tiphanie!"

Jackie Sue was running toward me from the back of the trailer park. She skidded up to me and grabbed ahold of my arm. "What are you doing here?" she said as she dragged me away from Clay.

"I came to meet you halfway, but you took too long so I kept walking." My heart was pounding a mile a minute, but the last thing I wanted to do was show Clay that he'd rattled me, so I tried to act normal. "So, you hungry? Mom's baked some cookies."

On the way to my house, I looked at Jackie Sue carefully. She seemed tired. Her green eyes were dimmer than usual and surrounded by dark circles.

"So what have you been doing to keep yourself busy without my charming company?" I asked.

"Nothing," she muttered. "And I really mean nothing. Was it nice to be back in your old neighborhood?"

I opened my mouth to tell her but shrugged instead. I could tell she was holding back something from me so I decided to hold back a little of the truth from her.

"Really, though," I said. "What did you do with all your time?"

"Nothing." After a silence that lasted a beat too long, Jackie Sue laughed softly. "No need to worry about me. I'm fine."

I tried to laugh along with her, but she still didn't look up, or truly answer my question.

That night, I overheard my parents talking outside my bedroom when they thought I was asleep.

"Well, she's made it through so far without any problems," my father said.

Ha, I thought to myself. *If they only knew.*

"Yes, she has," my mother answered. "Thank the good Lord I haven't had to go up there and cuss anyone out. Not even once."

Would Mom have cussed out Clay? I smiled into the darkness. She probably wouldn't have hit him in the head with her purse.

"Although I do have a few words I would like to say to that simple school secretary," my mother went on.

"Oh, Lord, help my wife," my father said in a reverend-like voice. "Help her to keep her mouth shut and not scare the white people."

They both laughed. Then my father said in a more serious tone, "I still worry, though. I know things aren't like they were when we were coming up, but the type of people who made our lives hard back in the day didn't disappear. They're still around."

"I know, honey. I shudder to think about what will happen when Tiphanie really gets a taste of how people can be. She's been lucky so far."

"Well, we'll cross that bridge when we come to it," my father said. "So far, so good. Let's not court trouble."

They went into their room and I lay there thinking about what they had said. For the most part my mom was right—I was lucky. Because even though there was no way to replace the friendships I'd left behind in my old neighborhood, I was no longer feeling alone and friendless.

The first thing Monday morning I was called into the vice principal's office. Walking slowly, I tried to figure out what had gotten me into trouble this time.

When I got to the office, Miss Tingle looked up at me with a frown. "Oh, my," she said. "We're here again?"

I frowned back at her. "Yes, ma'am, *we* are. I got a note to come to see Mr. Miller."

"Mr. Miller? Hmm. That's interesting. I'll let him know you're here."

Mr. Miller was an older man who hardly ever ventured into the hallways. I'd only seen him once before. "Ah yes, Miss Baker," he said as soon as I walked into his office. "It seems Mr. Ash believes you are breezing through his math class."

I sat down. "Um, I'm sorry?" I said.

"Math," Mr. Miller said. "Mr. Ash thinks you're in the wrong class." He pulled out a stack of papers that appeared to be my math homework. "After seeing your work, I would have to agree. This class is clearly far too easy for you. We will not allow our students to skate through classes that are below their capabilities. We have standards to meet. I've just finished talking with your mother, and as of today you are being moved up to a higher math class. Here's your new room assignment. Thank you." Mr. Miller handed me a paper and indicated that he was done with me.

So after English that day I wandered into my new honors algebra class. I was both excited and irritated at the turn of events. I was glad that I would get to move up to a more interesting class, but getting an easy A had its advantages too. I suppose I should have checked to see who the teacher was beforehand, though, because it turned out to be none other than Mrs. Steele. She snatched the transfer form out of my hand, read it with a grimace, and then pointed to a chair in the back of the room, despite the fact there were three or four empty ones closer to the front.

During class, I raised my hand to offer an answer to the quadratic equation Mrs. Steele had written on the board. But she didn't call on me, even though mine was the only hand raised. During the last twenty minutes of class she told us to turn to page 47 in our textbooks and work on the odd-numbered problems, and since I didn't have a textbook, my hand went up again. She still didn't call on me. Fortunately, Denise let me copy the problems out of her book.

After the bell rang, when I asked Mrs. Steele for a textbook, she stomped over to the cabinet, yanked out an old ratty copy, and thrust it into my hands. As I was leaving I saw her throw a paper into the trash basket by her desk that looked an awful lot like my classwork.

Even with her nasty attitude, I was still stunned when Mrs. Steele called my mother after school that day and requested a meeting. She said she didn't think this move was at all proper and was protesting it on my behalf. My mother arranged to meet with her before school the next day.

My mother was fuming all through dinner. "You know as well as I do that Tiphanie has always excelled in math," my mother told my father.

"Yes, that's true," he replied. "You can't assume anything, though. Go to the meeting and talk with this teacher before you lose your temper. This Mrs. Steele is probably a decent woman who means well."

I snorted. Mrs. Steele hardly meant well, but since I hadn't said anything to my parents about my previous run-in with her, I kept quiet.

The next morning Mom and I got to school a half hour before the first bell and met Mrs. Steele in the honors algebra room.

"Thank you for coming, Mrs. Baker," Mrs. Steele said. Her superior tone made me cringe. "I'm sure this meeting will be quick. I'd hate for you to get in trouble at work. It's never good to be late."

"It's no problem," my mother said. "I set my own hours."

"My, that must be nice. What exactly do you do? Clean houses? Nanny? Cook?"

"I'm a commercial real estate agent," my mom answered tersely.

Mrs. Steele seemed startled by that answer. "Oh, a professional. How nice. Well, let's get right to business, shall we? I'm concerned that in coming from a school district, in the, eh, the inner city, Tiphanie did not receive the foundation necessary to keep up in my accelerated algebra class, to which she was mistakenly reassigned. We go very quickly and many students, even my white students, have a hard time keeping pace. I have put in a request that she be placed back into the regular math class."

"You requested?" my mother said sharply. "I assumed that a decision like that would belong to the vice principal, or the parents."

I was just as angry as my mother. Mrs. Steele hadn't even given me a chance to fail. Or to succeed, for that matter.

"Yes, well, we teachers have a better feel for a student's ability than a mother has," Mrs. Steele said. "Experience, you know."

"And you are basing this decision on a single class period with Tiphanie?" my mother asked.

"It's a gut feeling I have. After so many years of teaching, I can judge students very quickly."

"Are you aware that it was her algebra teacher who suggested that we put Tiphanie in the honors class?"

"Be that as it may, Mr. Ash is quite young. I believe he's only been teaching for two or three years. I, on the other hand, have more than thirty years' experience, and I would hate to see Tiphanie fall behind and become frustrated because she is unable to keep up with the rest of the class."

"I am quite confident that my daughter can keep up in this class," my mother said. "Judging from her past academic performance, particularly in math, I expect my daughter to excel in your class, Mrs. Steele."

"There's no reason to get up in arms, Mrs. Baker," Mrs. Steele said. "Although I'm sure you *believe* Tiphanie is capable of keeping up, I have found that most mothers have an exaggerated idea of their own child's abilities. As an educator, I know what level of performance to expect from your type of child."

"My type of child, Mrs. Steele?" my mother barked, leaning forward in her chair. "What *type* of child do you believe she is?"

Mrs. Steele scooted her chair away from us and began fussing with her pearl necklace. "Well, to be frank, Mrs. Baker, I find that colored children usually aren't as prepared for school as the others are."

"Really, and how many *Black* children have you taught here?"

"That is not the point," Mrs. Steele responded primly, pulling on her necklace. "I'm simply trying to help you people."

"Yes, well thank you, but neither I nor Tiphanie, or any of *my* people for that matter, need your kind of help. Let's go, Tiphanie." My mother stood and strode toward the door, with me scurrying behind her.

Mrs. Steele looked taken aback at how the meeting had turned out. "Mrs. Baker, really, I am—"

"Mrs. Steele," my mother interrupted with a last look over her shoulder. "I know exactly what you are."

My mother marched me from Mrs. Steele's room right into the principal's office.

"I need to speak with Mr. Daniels immediately," she said to Miss Tingle.

Miss Tingle's eyes grew large at the tone of my mother's voice, but she turned and announced us. I followed my mother into his office.

"Good morning, Mrs. Baker," Mr. Daniels said. He stood and shook my mother's hand in the same two-handed manner he had shaken mine. "How may I help you?"

After my mother explained the situation, Mr. Daniels nodded calmly.

"Well, what we can do is have her take the standardized math placement test," he said. "If she places into honors algebra, I'm sure we will have no further problems convincing Mrs. Steele of Tiphanie's abilities."

"Fine." My mother was back to using her professional, real estate agent's voice, with a touch of warmth added in. "I want her to take it today."

"Yes, of course. Best to get it over with. Let's see. Tiphanie, what's your class schedule?" asked Mr. Daniels.

"First is English, then algebra, U.S. history, French . . ." I said, ticking them off on my fingers.

"Well, why don't we test her second period, instead of having her going to algebra?" Mr. Daniels suggested, buzzing for Miss Tingle.

"Thank you, Mr. Daniels," my mother said.

Mr. Daniels shook our hands again as we left his office. My mother gave me a pat on the back and hurried off to work. I went in search of Jackie Sue, hoping to talk to her before the bell rang so I could tell her how crazy my morning had been. But as it turned out, I didn't find her until later.

12

Second period I was deposited at a little desk hidden in the back of the school library with a standardized math test and two finely sharpened number two pencils. I had just started the test when I heard Jackie Sue's voice break the silence of the library.

"Would you get your hands off me, please?" she snapped.

I peeked over the desk and saw Clay walking in, dragging Jackie Sue behind him. That was strange, I thought. Why weren't they in class?

They both saw me at the same time. I gave Jackie Sue a wave, but the look on her face made me drop my hand instantly. She was either pissed to see me, or ashamed, I couldn't tell which. Clay continued to drag Jackie Sue along, pulling her behind some bookshelves.

I sat back down at my desk and stared at the test. There was a time limit and I really should have been focusing, but my curiosity got the best of me. What was going on between them? Why did Clay think he could boss her around? I peeked around my cubicle and, seeing that the coast was clear, got up and crept between the shelves in the direction that Jackie Sue and Clay had gone.

In the hush of the library, I could hear them whispering furiously. I tiptoed to the edge of the far row and hid behind the bookshelf, where I could make out their words more clearly.

"You don't own me, Clay," Jackie Sue was saying. "You can't tell me what to do or who I can talk to."

"Yeah, well, I figure that as long as you live at my dad's place rent-free you need to listen pretty close to me," Clay answered. "You're lucky I haven't told my dad what kind of riffraff you've been letting wander onto our property."

"We paid you last month," Jackie Sue hissed. "Just because we're a little late this time doesn't mean you get to—"

"Hey, it's not my fault your mess of a mom can't pay the rent on time," said Clay. "It's a good thing my dad is so nice, otherwise you'd be out on the streets. You want to hang out with Negroes, fine. But I suggest you find somewhere else to live."

"Excuse me!" The librarian was heading over to them. "Shouldn't you two be in class?"

I hustled as quickly as I could back to my cubby. Then I sat at my desk for a few minutes trying to fill in the blanks of what I'd heard, before I realized I needed to get back to work on my test. At least answering the questions on the math test would be easier than answering the questions I had about Jackie Sue's life.

I didn't see Jackie Sue the rest of the day. Not at lunch and not in home ec. I couldn't get her conversation with Clay out of my mind. I had finally realized what the look on Jackie Sue's face was whenever she saw Clay—it was the look of a trapped animal.

My mother pounced on me as soon as I walked through the door that afternoon. She must have come home early so she could harass me about my math test.

"Well, how did it go? Was it difficult? Did you try your best?"

"It went fine," I said. "It wasn't too hard." I only answered her first two questions, because I knew that answering the last one would force me to lie.

"Good. I'm sure you knocked the test out of the park. I can't wait to rub your scores in that woman's face tomorrow. You're part of the movement now, Tiphanie. Your test scores will lay a path for others to follow. I'm going to make you some of your favorite cinnamon rolls for dinner to celebrate."

As my mother hustled into the kitchen, I collapsed onto the sofa. Over the sound of the bowls and dishes banging in the kitchen, I could hear my mother phoning family members and telling them about what happened today at school. "Girl, please," she was saying. "You know Tiphanie and math. That woman will be sorry she even opened her mouth. My little girl will show her."

All of a sudden, I was panicked. That morning the test hadn't seemed like such a big deal, but now I realized it meant more to my parents than simply figuring out which math class I was supposed to be in. The way my mother was talking, it was as if I took the test to prove something for my entire race.

When my mother finally finished calling everyone in her phone book, I raced to the phone and called Jackie Sue. I needed to talk to my best friend.

"Hello?" slurred a voice.

"Uh, Jackie Sue," I said. "Is that you?"

"She ain't here." Then the line was disconnected. When I tried to call again later the line was busy.

I could barely eat my breakfast the next morning because my stomach was tied in so many knots. Why hadn't I focused on the test instead of spying on Clay and Jackie Sue? What if I proved Mrs. Steele right? And why hadn't Jackie Sue told me what was going on in the first place? Then I wouldn't have had to spy on her!

For the second day in a row, my mother and I arrived at school early. We had a meeting with Mr. Daniels and Mrs. Steele to discuss the results of the test.

"Well, thank you all for coming here so early," Mr. Daniels began. "I'm sure that the results will clear up this little misunderstanding."

"Yes, Mr. Daniels. We're anxious to hear the results so we can adjust Tiphanie's schedule accordingly." My mother's voice sounded calm, but her hands were clutching at her purse.

"Well," Mr. Daniels said, "Tiphanie did not place into Mrs. Steele's honors algebra class."

My breakfast came up to my mouth. I could feel the dismay coming off my mother in waves.

Mrs. Steele was smiling and preening like a peacock. "Yes, well, I'm not at all surprised," she said smugly. "As I was trying to tell Mrs. Baker yesterday about the education of colored—"

Mr. Daniels interrupted her. "Tiphanie actually placed *out* of ninth grade honors algebra and into an even higher level," he said. "Does *that* surprise you, Mrs. Steele?" Mr. Daniels was beaming at me, his eyes twinkling. My mother began grinning hysterically. "Not only that," he continued, "but she scored into *eleventh* grade honors trigonometry. So, Mrs. Steele, I'm sure she would have been fine in your class. In fact, it may have been a wee bit easy for her." Mr. Daniels looked so pleased, it was as if he'd taken the test himself.

"Yes, well . . ." sputtered Mrs. Steele. Her hand clutched at her pearl necklace. "Are you sure she was alone in the library? Perhaps another student—"

My mother interrupted her with a dismissive wave of her hand. "Mr. Daniels, do you think it would be possible for Tiphanie to take a higher level of math this year?"

Mr. Daniels scanned a sheet of paper. "Yes, I'd suggest we put her in the advanced tenth grade class, honors geometry. Just to make sure she has a really tight foundation. Then next year when she's a sophomore we can put her into honors trig. It looks like Mr. Hoops's honors geometry class is second period as well, so there's no need to juggle the rest of Tiphanie's schedule around to accommodate the change. All this has been quite serendipitous. Mrs. Baker, I just need your John Hancock on the bottom of this form, and we are all set."

I turned to Mrs. Steele. "Thank you so much, Mrs. Steele," I said politely. "If you hadn't said anything, I wouldn't have had this opportunity."

"Yes, indeed," my mother added. "Thank you, Mrs. Steele. I guess that thirty years' experience of yours is useful for something." She turned and gave me a tight hug. "I couldn't be prouder of you, Tiphanie," she said. "You've done us all proud!"

Mrs. Steele opened her mouth as if to protest one last time, but Mr. Daniels spoke first.

"I, for one, think that anyone with more than thirty years' experience would be thinking seriously about retirement, Mrs. Steele," he said. "Surely it must have crossed your mind."

Mrs. Steele scowled at Mr. Daniels and without a word stood up, spun on her heel, and left the office.

As my mother and I walked toward the door, I could have sworn I heard Mr. Daniels mutter, "Crusty old bat."

I walked happily to my locker and was pleased to find Jackie Sue leaning against it. I could tell right away that she was in a bad mood, but I was too happy to care.

"Hey!" I said, gently pushing her out of the way so I could open my locker. "I called you like fifty times last night! Where the heck were you? You won't believe what's been happening to me. What a trip!"

Jackie Sue shrugged but didn't say a word.

"Not to mention that I had to eat lunch all alone yesterday," I whined.

"Poor Tiphanie, life must be very hard for you."

I opened my mouth to zing her back, but a picture of Clay and Jackie Sue in the library flashed into my head. Did he really have the power to kick her out of her house? And was her being friends with me adding to the problem? Jackie Sue looked awful, as if she hadn't slept at all, and I realized that she was wearing the same thing she had on yesterday.

"You missed a riveting discussion about the value of embroidering aprons in home ec," I said, attempting to get a smile out of her. "It was quite, um, let's see, what's a word you would understand? *Enlightening.*"

"I don't care," Jackie Sue mumbled.

"Come on, don't be so grumpy," I said. I reached over, spun her around, and rubbed her shoulders.

"Grumpy?" she replied, craning her neck to see me. "Try morose, despondent, disconsolate, and melancholy."

"Nah, I'm pretty sure the dwarf you are is Grumpy," I told her. She started to smile, but then her eyes flitted over my shoulder and she grimaced instead.

"Gotta go to class, see ya at lunch," she said, hurrying away from me. Turning, I saw Clay coming down the hall. I slammed my locker shut and began walking to English, my head buzzing with questions. For someone I thought of as my best friend, sometimes—a lot of times—Jackie Sue felt like a stranger to me.

13

Halloween—and Troy's party—was that coming Friday, but as hard as I tried to convince Jackie Sue to go with me, she kept saying she wasn't up for it. Finally I decided that if Jackie Sue wouldn't go, then neither would I. Sure, the science project guys were going to be there, but if any of the elaborate plans that they had been plotting in science class worked, then they would be off in a corner of Troy's basement, making out with their dream girls.

Friday evening, while I was busy handing out tiny Snickers bars, the door rang for the twentieth time. My parents had put me on candy duty while they were in the den watching the evening news. Imagine my surprise when on the other side of the door I found Jackie Sue, in full costume.

"Trick or treat," she said, stepping out of the way of a gang of kids coming up behind her with their bags open. "Is that what you're wearing?" she asked as she helped me distribute candy bars to a miniature Six Million Dollar Man, a tiny Wonder Woman, and a braided Laura Ingalls.

"What do you mean?" I asked, looking down at my ratty jeans and shirt. Jackie Sue was wearing a long, fancy emerald green dress, with a sash that said MISS NORTHEAST ALABAMA on it, and she was carrying a scepter. Her reddish blond hair was pulled up into an elaborate curly beehive hairdo, topped off by an elegant tiara.

"Is that the costume you're wearing to the party?"

"I thought we weren't going." I closed the door, only for the bell to ring five seconds later. "I mean, just today you told me you didn't want to go."

"Well, I don't really want to, but you looked so melancholy in home ec today, not to mention the sulking and sighing you were doing on the way home. So I thought I'd take pity on you and go. I even brought a change of clothes so I can spend the night after. I can be magnanimous when I feel like it. But if you don't want to go, fine with me. I'm happy handing out candy to all these Planet of the Apes, Fonzies, and Josie and the Pussycats clones."

"Magna-what?" I asked. "Never mind, it doesn't matter anyway. I can't go. I didn't buy a costume."

"Go make one. Be a bum or something, that's always easy. The party doesn't start till, what? Seven? You've got time," Jackie Sue said. "I'll give out candy while you figure it out." Then she shooed me away to my bedroom and returned to handing out Tootsie Rolls.

I needed something cute. Jackie Sue looked amazing and I didn't want to be outdone. After some frantic thinking, I dug into the back of my closet and pulled out one of the pairs of pink footie pajamas that my grandma insisted on sending me each Christmas. Who knew where she got them in size seven teen, but I hadn't worn them so they were fresh out of the package. I got out the brand-new white wool hat that my mother had just bought me for the coming winter, cut off the big fluffy pom-pom on top, and managed to sew it on the back of the pink pajamas. I guess home ec wasn't useless after all.

I grabbed a couple of hangers, some felt and glue, and after a bit of struggle I created two pink bunny ears. It took me a half hour and half a box of bobby pins to figure out how to get the ears to stay on my head. Then, with my mom's makeup, I drew on a black nose and some whiskers and added a little lipstick for the heck of it. I grinned at myself in the mirror. Not bad on short notice.

I walked downstairs in my bunny costume. Jackie Sue was still standing at the door holding our candy basket, but now she was talking with my mother. She looked relieved to see me come into the room.

"I know, Mrs. Baker, we've been quite remiss in our societal obligations," Jackie Sue was saying. "I will definitely tell my mother. It's just that it's difficult for her to . . . get off work."

My mother nodded, looking intently at Jackie Sue. "I understand. I imagine it is quite hard for her to raise you alone. However, we've had the pleasure of your company for weeks and we have yet to meet your mother. I would love to have her over for dinner. I realize she works the night shift, but she surely must have a night off every once in a while. And she's got to eat, right? You tell her to check her schedule and let us know when a good time is and we'll set it all up. Perhaps I should get your telephone number from Tiphanie and call her myself. That might be more polite."

Jackie Sue's eyes widened in alarm. "No, no!" she almost shouted. "No, I better tell her!"

My mother's eyebrows shot up.

"It's just that, well, since she works so much, when she's off she really has to catch up on her sleep and I usually unplug the phone so she's not disturbed," Jackie Sue explained, her voice beginning to return to a normal volume. "She's really, um, cranky, when her sleep is disrupted."

"Yes, of course, of course," my mother said. "Well, you talk to her then and just let us know. Morris and I are anxious to meet the woman who has raised such a well-spoken young lady." Jackie Sue nodded, and my mom finally turned her attention to me. "Well, that's a cute costume, sweetie. Very clever." I spun around and modeled it for her. "Where did you get that fluffy tail?"

"Oh, it's from some winter hat that was lying around," I answered, grabbing a coat and edging toward the door.

"Slow down," my mother said. "Where exactly is this party?"

"It's at Troy Weingard's house. It's only two or three blocks away, 2201 South Melody Drive. Daddy knows his father. I guess Mr. Weingard got a big loan or something from Daddy's bank." I put my hand on the doorknob. "The party ends at ten so we'll be home by ten-fifteen or so. Can

Jackie Sue spend the night?" I pulled the door open to find more Wonder Women and yet another tiny Fonzie. Jackie Sue escaped out onto our porch.

"Of course she may. You two be careful walking over there and back, especially back. Actually, maybe your father should come and pick you up."

"Oh, Mom, we can walk home," I whined. "There are a thousand people out." A lecture was coming; I could feel it. It was time to go.

"Yes, I know, but your father picking you up is a better idea. He'll be there at ten to get you ladies—2201 South Melody Drive. Now, Tiphanie, I need you to be on your best behavior this evening. This is the first time you've been invited to one of your classmates' parties and I must stress the importance of acting polite and proper. Your behavior reflects not only on this family, but on the entire race as well."

I inched out the door, nodding my head, my bunny ears flopping.

"Yes, Mom, I know. Really, I do. I'll be a fine upstanding member of my race, really I will. We better be going. Don't want to be late and reinforce any stereotypes! Love you! Bye!" I dashed past the trick-or-treaters to meet Jackie Sue.

On our way to Troy's, as we dodged the gangs of kids on candy highs, Jackie Sue walked very carefully, holding her gown with one hand and carrying her scepter with the other. I began to regret my choice of costumes. She looked like a princess. I looked like a pet.

"What was that conversation you were having with my mom about?" I asked her.

Jackie Sue stepped daintily over a pile of leaves. "She wants to have my mother over for dinner. But it's a bad idea." The way her face was set I knew I wouldn't get any more information out of her.

"Maybe I should have worn something else," I said, changing the subject. "Where did you get that stuff anyway?"

Jackie Sue shrugged. "It was lying around my house."

"A scepter, tiara, ball gown, and sash were lying around your house?" I asked.

She stopped just as we reached Troy's house and looked over at me appraisingly. "You look cute. You know, you really are quite curvy. I hadn't noticed before, but you're shaped like a Coca-Cola bottle."

"You think?" I asked, holding my coat open and studying myself in the reflection of one of Troy's front windows.

"Yes, dear. You're filling out nicely," Jackie Sue said with a laugh. She pushed the doorbell.

"Oh shut up," I said, laughing along.

The door opened. Judging by her open-mouth stare, Mrs. Weingard was a bit stunned to see me. "Uh, hello there. Are you here for Troy's party?" she asked.

"Yes, ma'am," Jackie Sue and I said in unison.

Mrs. Weingard's eyebrows twitched up slightly, but she said politely, "Oh, fine. Please follow me."

In the front room, Mr. Weingard was watching *Sanford and Son*. My parents hated that show—they were always going on about "buffoonish behavior masquerading as cultural comedy," or something like that. Personally, I didn't see the big deal. I thought it was just a silly show about an old man and his son living in a junkyard.

"Hello, Mr. Weingard," I said, walking toward him with my hand outstretched. "I'm Tiphanie Baker. I believe you know my father, Morris Baker—he works at Colorado National Bank."

Mr. Weingard looked surprised at my formality, but rose to shake my hand. "Yes, I sure do know your father. Stand-up guy, quite a businessman. Pleasure to meet you," he said.

Jackie Sue held out her hand too. "Hi, I'm Jackie Sue Webster," she said.

"Nice to meet you as well," Mr. Weingard greeted her. "I must say, you two are very well raised. Those other kids marched right through here as if I didn't exist at all. It's a relief to know that my son is acquainted with a few kids who possess some manners. Have fun, gals."

Mrs. Weingard ushered us down the stairs to the rec room, then returned up the stairs, closing the door behind her.

Jackie Sue and I stood at the bottom of the stairs, taking everything in. There were bats and spiderwebs hanging from the ceiling, and half a dozen expertly carved pumpkins lighting up the room. A huge bowl full of bloodred punch was surrounded by candy and popcorn balls, and "Monster Mash" was playing on the stereo.

We caught sight of the science group huddled over by the couch, and when Troy noticed us he waved us over. I pulled Jackie Sue along with me. We walked past the Barbies, who all had the same cheerleading costume on—Joanie Cunningham's blue and yellow outfit from *Happy Days*—with blue and yellow ribbons in their blond ponytails. It was a little creepy. And stupid, since Joanie was a brunette. As we walked by, I heard one of them mutter, "Look how they just go right over to them."

"Hey, guys," I said as they made room for Jackie Sue and me. "What are we doing? Planning our next play? I say we go long."

"Ha, ha, ha," Troy said miserably. "My party's lame. It's like we're still in junior high. I gotta do something."

I looked around. Troy was right. There were clumps of kids all over the room, standing in their usual cliques, looking at each other uncertainly.

"Yeah, this blows, man," said Andy. "Let's bag it and go trick-or-treating. Or better yet, let's just snatch some candy from a few little kids."

"What's the problem?" I asked, ignoring Andy. "All your little would-be girlfriends are here." I pointed to the refreshment table, where Denise was munching on M&M's. She was dressed as Jeannie, from *I Dream of Jeannie*, and Gretchen was there too, as Bo Peep. Holly, a girl who had a not-so-secret crush on Bradley, was wearing a gold lamé dress with a few dozen miniature carrots stuck on it. "Why don't you just go over and talk to them?"

"And say what?" Steve asked pathetically. " 'Are those M&M's good?' "

"Oh, for heaven's sake," I said. "How about saying 'nice costume' or something like that?"

"Oh yeah, like *that* would work," Andy said. "Then what?"

I turned to Jackie Sue for assistance, but she was looking up at the basement door, where Mrs. Weingard was escorting more people into the party. Among them were Clay, dressed as a mummy, and Grant, as Dracula. Jackie Sue sighed.

"Let's see," I said, turning my attention back to the boys. "Since talking to the girls seems to be out, how about dancing?"

"Dancing? I can't dance!" Steve moaned. He started flailing about to the monster music. "See?"

"Oh dear Lord, please stop that," I said. "I was actually talking about slow dancing, but if you guys—"

"Wait!" Bradley interrupted, looking excited. "That could work. You don't have to talk with slow dancing, and there's touching involved. Watch." He grabbed my arm and pulled me to my feet.

Bradley flung his arms over my shoulders and started moving his feet slowly from side to side. I put my hands on his waist and followed his steps.

"Check it out!" he said, letting go of me. "Nothing to it."

I was pretty sure that the girl's arms were supposed to be on top and the boy's hands around the waist, but I didn't want to mention it since the boys looked so relieved.

Bradley raced over to the stereo. The monster music was suddenly gone and in its place Earth, Wind & Fire's "Reasons" started to play.

The girls began giggling and whispering to each other. And the boys stood there.

"Oh for goodness' sake," I said. I went over to the wall

and turned off the light, so that the room was lit only by the glowing pumpkins. Then I walked behind Troy and pushed him toward Denise.

"Okay, okay," he muttered, twisting away from me. He took a deep breath, walked over, and asked her to dance. Next I gave Steve a push toward Gretchen. "I'm going, I'm going," he whispered over his shoulder. "Stop shoving, I'm going!" I looked at Bradley and put my hands on my hips. He shook his head with a smile and headed to Holly.

Before long the floor was filled with couples slowly rocking back and forth. I mentally patted myself on the back, took some M&M's from the refreshment table, and looked around for Jackie Sue. I didn't see her anywhere.

Jackie Sue had ditched me.

14

Maybe I was being paranoid, I thought. I grabbed another handful of M&M's and was looking around again for Jackie Sue when someone from behind me said, "Hey, uh, Tip, um, Tiphanie?"

I turned and saw Todd standing in front of me. He was staring at his feet. My stomach filled with butterflies.

"Hey, Todd," I said, tossing an M&M in my mouth, trying to be cool. But the candy flew straight down my throat, making me gag.

Todd pounded me on my back. "Whoa. You okay?"

"Yeah, I'm cool," I said through coughs.

"So, doyouwanttodance?"

"Yes! I mean, did you just ask me to dance?" I leaned in closer to him. Better make sure.

"Yes, do you wanna?"

"Sure." I turned around and tried to find a napkin to put the rest of my M&M's on, but it was too dark to see. I turned back around and saw Todd standing on the edge of the dance floor, waiting for me. I hurried over to him, keeping my hand tightly clenched around the M&M's, and put my hands—well, my hand and my M&M-filled fist—on his waist.

"Um, Todd," I whispered. "Todd!"

He was quite a bit taller than I was, and I felt a little silly stepping side to side on my tiptoes like a ballerina.

"I think your hands are supposed to be on my waist and my arms on your shoulders," I said.

He stopped dancing. "Really?" he asked. He put his arms very gently around my waist, and I raised my hands and rested them on his shoulders, relieved to have the weight of his arms off my own. Then we danced in one very, very slow circle until the song ended.

The lights came on, and Troy and Bradley rushed over to the stereo, frantically trying to find another record.

That's when I saw Clay again.

"Dang, Todd, I thought you were dancing all alone," he sneered, walking over to Todd and me. "Your little partner there is so dark I don't know how you can even see her with the lights out. Tiphanie, maybe you could try smiling next time, so Todd can keep track of you."

I heard a couple of snickers scattered about the room.

"I know you like chocolate, Todd," Clay continued. "But really, enough is enough."

"Shut up, Clay," Todd muttered. But he said it so quietly I didn't think anyone heard him except me.

That's it? I thought. *Shut up?* So much for having a knight in shining armor by my side. Time to save myself. "Do *you* like chocolate?" I asked Clay, taking a step forward. "Here. Have some." I took my M&M hand and wiped it on his mummy costume, smearing green, red, and brown candy shells and melted chocolate down his front. "Mummies always say to share." I smiled as I heard stronger, more widespread laughter behind me.

"Why you little nig—" Clay started.

"Watch yourself, Clay!" Bradley said, coming over from the stereo to stand beside me. "I strongly suggest you don't finish that word."

At that moment, Queen's "Bohemian Rhapsody" started up, and the couples rushed back to the dance floor, too eager to get back in each other's arms to care about anything else. Clay glared at me before stalking off.

Todd gestured vaguely toward the dance floor, but I just frowned at him. I was suddenly seeing him in a new light.

"I better go wash up first," I said. I held out my hand which was now a mess of smeared chocolate and bits of candy shells. Melt in your mouth and not in your hand, my foot. "This song is like an hour long. I'll be back, 'kay?"

The bathroom was on the other side of the basement but the door was locked. I waited for ages, but the door didn't open. Finally I gave up and headed toward the basement stairs, figuring I'd use the sink in the kitchen. On my way through the dance floor, it was so dark that I bumped directly into a dancing couple.

"Oh, sorry," I said. I looked up to see Todd and Gretchen with their arms around each other, dancing much closer than he and I had been. I guess there hadn't been a need to hurry.

Todd obviously wasn't waiting for me. For a moment I stood rooted to the spot. The three of us stared at each other.

"I gotta . . . er, I mean, I gotta find the kitchen," I finally muttered.

After washing my hands, I headed back downstairs and wandered over to the food table, grabbed some more M&M's, and watched as the couples paired up to dance to a new song, this time "Stairway to Heaven." It seemed my idea was working, at least for everyone else.

I sat down on the couch, and Bradley came over to sit beside me.

"Hey, Tip, having a good time?" he asked.

"Oh, yeah," I said. "Just a fab time." Where was Jackie Sue anyway? I didn't see her anywhere.

Bradley must have thought I was looking over at Todd and Gretchen, who were still slow-dancing directly in front of us.

"I know how you must feel. Look, I know you like Todd, and he likes you. He's told me. But you gotta know that he's not the type who can really deal with the pressure of hanging with you, you dig?" He said this softly, as if he was scared to hurt my feelings by telling me the harsh truth.

"Yeah, I get it, Bradley, really. It's okay," I said. "Really, I'm cool with it." And I was. My crush on Todd had melted away the minute he hadn't stood up to Clay for me anyway. I guess it hadn't been all that serious to begin with.

"Well, stop looking so freaked out then," Bradley said. "Not having a boyfriend isn't the end of the world." He patted my shoulder and headed back to the stereo.

I stayed on the couch until Jackie Sue finally appeared an eternity later. She came over and sat down next to me with a plop.

"Where have you been?" I asked her.

"In the bathroom, trying to avoid Clay," she told me, rolling her eyes. "He's been harassing me since he got here."

That made two of us.

Finally, at 9:50, Mrs. Weingard came down to announce that a father had come to pick up someone. The party disbanded, and we all grabbed our coats and headed outside to wait for our rides. Jackie Sue stood next to me, shivering in her old, thin winter coat.

Off in the distance a firecracker went off, causing several of us girls to jump and shriek in surprise.

"What's the matter, Tiphanie?" Clay said. "Aren't you used to hearing things that sound like shotguns? Or have you seen a ghost or something?"

"She's hasn't seen a ghost, man," Grant replied. "She *is* a ghost. Our own little school spook."

"Hey, not cool!" Denise shouted. "Totally bogus statement, Grant. You're such a spaz. Don't pay any attention to them, Tip."

I smiled at Denise, grateful that she'd stood up for me. But when I looked over at Jackie Sue, she was staring off down the block, like she hadn't even heard what Clay had said. I knew Clay had been giving her a lot of trouble lately, but as my friend wasn't it her job to stand up for me anyway? I would have for her.

I was just working myself into a real angry huff, when

Jackie Sue suddenly took a step forward and pointed at Clay's head. "With ears like yours," she said, "I would think you'd have dressed like the jackass you are, instead of a mummy. That way you could have saved your dad's sheet for your Klan hood."

Clay glared at her in disbelief, and Jackie Sue stared back at him with defiance in her eyes. Right then my dad pulled up, and not a minute too soon.

Jackie Sue and I should have been happy when we got back to my house. We should have been giggling and gossiping about who danced with whom. Instead we silently prepared for bed, both of us lost in our own thoughts. We pulled out my trundle bed and turned off the lights without saying a word to each other. I lay there listening to her breathing, knowing that down on the trundle she was wide awake too.

"Have I ever told you about Ohatchee?" Jackie Sue said finally.

I rolled over to face in her direction. "What's Ohatchee?"

"Ohatchee, Alabama. It's where I'm from."

"Alabama, really? No, you haven't." I had no idea where she was from. I was beginning to realize that there were a lot of things concerning Jackie Sue I didn't know.

Jackie Sue sighed and was silent for a while before finally saying, "We had a house back in Ohatchee. It wasn't big, but it was pretty. And we owned a little bit of land—more than an acre. There was a beautiful oak tree in the back, with a tire swing. There was a creek too." Her voice was wistful. "Not like here. We've got nothing here. We *are* nothing."

"You aren't nothing, Jackie Sue," I said.

Jackie Sue was quiet again.

"So why did you leave?" I asked. I reached over and turned on my lava lamp and the room took on a cozy glow—lighter, but still too dim for us to be able to see each other's expressions clearly.

I heard Jackie Sue shifting around. "You asked about all the stuff I had on tonight? The evening gown and the tiara? All that crap belongs to my mom. She did a lot of pageants down south. Won a lot of them, actually. She'd always dreamed of being a big country singing star. She was going to win the Miss America contest and get a big recording contract. Then she got pregnant with me. Of course, after I was born she shoved me into pageants before I could even sit up. Miss Beautiful Baby, Little Miss Alabama, Southern Baby Starlet, Little Miss SweetPea, Miss Magnolia Baby. God, there were so many of them. I hated them."

Jackie Sue stopped talking for another long minute, clearly lost in her memories. I waited. "I don't really know who my daddy is," she said, so softly that I almost didn't hear her. "But when I was ten my mom started seeing this new guy, a young judge from one of the pageants. I guess it was a big scandal in the pageant world and people wouldn't let it die. Anyway, Mom decided we should leave Alabama— begin a new life out west. Start clean and fresh, make our way to Hollywood. So Mom sells the house and the land, and we get as far as Colorado when her boyfriend, who it turns out was already married, gets homesick, or wife-sick, or whatever. So he up and leaves. Goes back to his wife and kids. And he takes our money with him. Not some or half of the money, all of it. We tried to get it back but we didn't have anything for a lawyer, and Mom's never been too good with stuff like that. So here we are, stuck in Colorado, with no money and with no place to live. Nothing. My mom has a sister, but they haven't talked in years, and Mom refused to call her for help. Said she'd been the shame of the family too many times. So we were all alone. Finally, Mom gets a job at this oil company which pays decent, and I think, well, okay, things will start to get better. She moves us into the trailer park and meets Clay's dad, who's this nasty old redneck, just like Clay, and she starts going out to bars at night with him. First it was only on Saturday nights, and then it was Friday *and* Saturday nights. After a while it was just about every night of the week. I would stay up so late, sometimes, looking out our window, waiting for her to come home."

Jackie Sue paused again. I stayed silent. The picture she was painting was so foreign to me, I couldn't think of anything to say.

"Well, then my mom, she loses her job, but Clay's dad says we can live in the park rent-free. And that was fine, I guess, until my mom and Clay's dad broke up. And Mom can't seem to find another job, because her reading isn't all that great and she sucks at numbers. She doesn't even have her high school diploma. She's lost I don't know how many jobs because she can't run a register without screwing up the drawer. All she really had going for her were her looks and her voice and now she spends so much time drinking that those don't do her much good anymore."

Through the dim light I saw Jackie Sue swipe at her face. "I don't like Clay, Tiphanie. But we're still living at the trailer park and since we can hardly pay the rent he thinks he has control over me or something. I'm pretty sure the only reason we haven't been kicked out already is because Clay has a crush on me. So now he thinks he can tell me who to talk to and who to be friends with. He keeps saying that Mom and I will have to live out on the streets if I don't do what he says. And he's right."

"But, Jackie Sue, there's gotta be a way to fix things," I said finally.

"Yeah, what?"

I searched my brain for an answer. "I don't know. Maybe my mom and dad can help," I suggested. "Loan you guys some money so you can move out of the trailer park."

Jackie Sue bolted upright. "No! Please don't tell them, Tip." Her voice was suddenly tense. "It's stuff like this that gets kids taken from their parents. Then where would I go? Some foster home? What would my mom do without me?"

"But maybe my parents could—" I started to say.

"No! I'm not a charity case! Swear to me that you won't say a word to anyone. Give me your solemn vow." Jackie Sue held out her pinky finger to me. I opened my mouth to respond, but she said quietly, "Once I can get my mom to stop drinking, she'll find a job she can do. Then things will be all right. This is just a rough patch we're going through. I can handle it. We'll be fine. Please, promise me."

Part of me wanted to tell an adult who could help—my mom, my dad, a teacher. Someone. But another part of me wanted to take the easy way out, the route that Jackie Sue was asking me—pleading with me—to take. And even though I knew it was the wimpy way out, it was what my friend, my best friend, was asking me to do.

So I leaned over and offered her my pinky. She hooked hers onto mine and we shook.

"I promise not to tell," I said quietly.

"No matter what," she added.

I hesitated.

"No matter what," she repeated, gripping my pinky so hard it hurt.

"Yeah, of course," I said. "No matter what."

She released my finger. "Thank you, Tiphanie," she whispered.

I didn't answer. Suddenly I felt as if the burden that Jackie Sue had been carrying alone was on my shoulders too, and I didn't want it there.

November 1975

The Company You Keep Lecture

*A*nd another thing. Why haven't we met Jackie Sue's parents yet? We need to know her people. To know her people is to know her better. The apple does not fall far from the tree. I honestly don't see why this is such an unusual request. Especially since you two spend so much time together.

Your father and I worked hard to put you in a position to succeed. You have more opportunities than anyone in our family's history. Don't mess it up by choosing the wrong friends. As a Black girl you must always be mindful of the company you keep, Tiphanie. Whether you like it or not, your friends are a reflection upon you.

15

The next morning both Jackie Sue and I were quiet and preoccupied, as if the conversation the night before had drained us. We got dressed and lounged around my room until my mother called us down for breakfast.

"So," Mom said, "how was the party?"

"Fine," Jackie Sue and I answered in unison.

"Did you behave yourselves?" my father asked. "Did you introduce yourself properly to Troy's parents?"

"Yes, sir," I said. "He said you were a stand-up guy, or something like that."

"So what did you do?" my mother asked. "Dance, play games?"

I opened my mouth to answer, but realized that the true answer was, Sit on the couch, watching everyone else dance and have fun, and stuff myself with M&M's until I felt sick. So I answered, "You know. The usual."

"So were there any other . . ." My father stopped mid-sentence with a glance toward Jackie Sue.

"Yes, Daddy," I said. "Bradley Jepperson was there."

He nodded, satisfied, and started in on his eggs.

Jackie Sue took off right after breakfast, and I spent the bulk of the day in my room doing homework, avoiding my mother. I wasn't in the mood to answer her prying questions about the party, and I knew that if she happened to ask the right ones I would probably spill my guts and tell her all the secrets I promised Jackie Sue I'd keep. It was best that I stay in my room and pretend that all was well.

Sunday morning I still wasn't myself, and apparently it was noticeable.

"So what is going on between you and Jackie Sue?" my mom asked in the car on the way to church. "She took off much sooner than usual. I was expecting to see her all day Saturday. Did something happen at the Halloween party? Did you two have a falling-out?"

"We were tired," I said. "We stayed up too late and you didn't let us sleep in any at all." I was hoping to throw her off the scent by putting the blame on her.

"Well," she said, turning back around to look at me, "when we get home you'll need to get me Jackie Sue's number so I can invite her and her mother to dinner."

"Oh, Mom," I moaned.

"*Oh, Mom,* what?" she snapped. "I have broken bread with every single one of your friends' parents your entire life. Why should Jackie Sue and her mother be any different? I mean, is it a race thing?"

"It's just that . . ." I started. "I mean, it's . . . Maybe you . . ."

"What, Tiphanie Jayne?" my mother asked.

"Mrs. Webster works a lot and she's always real tired, you know?"

"Well, *you've* met her, haven't you?"

"She's raising Jackie Sue alone, Mom," I answered, ignoring her question. "She used to be a beauty queen."

"So you're saying she's pretty," my mom answered. "That doesn't tell me too much about what she's like as a person, Tip. What is she like?"

I cast frantically around in my mind, trying to fish up some truth, or at the very least a half-truth to tell my mother. "Well, she's from Alabama," I said.

"She's from the deep south?" muttered my dad. "Oh, Lord."

"Well, then we definitely need to meet her," my mom said.

My dad nodded in agreement. "Where does she work?"

I shifted uncomfortably in my seat. Why was it taking so long to get to church? I wished my dad would drive faster.

"Oh, well, I think she worked, er, she works, at an oil company," I lied.

"I thought Jackie Sue mentioned that she works a lot of nights," my mother said.

Whoops.

"Oh, well, I think she must have two jobs. Jackie Sue's not rich like most of my classmates, you know."

"Yes, we gathered that," my father said.

"Well, that doesn't mean she's not as good as them," I said. "She's been a good friend to me. Besides, being poor isn't a crime. Are we better people now that we're rich?"

I saw my mother give my father a sidelong glance which he silently answered with a raised eyebrow.

"We aren't saying that there's anything wrong with being poor," my mother said slowly. "It's clear that Jackie Sue isn't as well situated as the bulk of the people in the neighborhood, but that doesn't mean she's a bad person."

"Well, it sounded like you were putting her down for being poor. Jesus was poor, you know. Would he have been a better savior if he had been 'better situated'? I mean, the rich guys in the Bible aren't all that great, you know."

My dad parked in the church parking lot and I hopped out of the car quickly. "I'm going to find my friends and head to Sunday school, okay?"

As I turned and walked—fled—away from my parents, they sat in the car, looking surprised. For the first time in my life I'd lectured them into speechlessness. It was a pretty good feeling.

Regina was the only one in the Sunday school room when I got there.

"What up?" I said, plopping down in the seat next to her.

"Just waiting for the always late Mrs. Taylor," she said. "What up with you? You look a little freaked."

"Oh, my parents were being bogus," I muttered. I started digging through my purse for some gum.

Regina laughed. "Um, bogus? You know we don't really

say that here in the hood. That must be some suburban white people slang."

"Please don't start with that," I snapped.

"Whoa, chill, okay?"

"Yeah, well, every time I see you guys now it's 'Your hair's this. You're talking white that. Blah, blah, blah.' I'm sick of it." Regina was looking at me as if I'd lost my mind. "I live around all white people now. So I pick up a few new slang words. That doesn't mean I'm trying to be white, or trying not to be Black. I'm still me. Is that all right with you? Or should I say, 'Can ya dig it?' Would that make it clearer to you?"

By this time Simon, Simone, and Joseph had arrived. I didn't know how much of my rant they'd heard, but Joseph said, "Yeah, we can dig it. We've just been playing with you. You're a cool chick. I mean, my mom and I are going to move soon . . ."

The attention in the room turned toward Joseph.

"Where to?" I asked.

"Oh, you know, out to Aurora," Joseph answered, not sounding at all like his usual defiant self. "My mom got a promotion."

"Oh, Lordy, looks like we're going to have another Oreo to deal with," Simon said.

"Boy, shut up," I said quickly.

Aurora wasn't technically a suburb, but it definitely wasn't the hood either. It seemed Joseph would soon be seeing the world a little differently too.

"Yeah, Simon," Joseph told him. "You talk too much.

Just give me a reason to help you learn how to keep your big mouth shut."

"Ohh, looky, the male Oreo's getting mad," Simone added. "Let's get a giant glass of milk, dunk him, and help him cool off."

Just as Joseph opened his mouth, undoubtedly to say something about how Simon had earned himself a beat-down, Mrs. Taylor waltzed in.

"You young people are being entirely too loud," she scolded us. "In your seats, please. Thank you. Now, today's lesson is from 1 Samuel 16:7. 'But the Lord said to Samuel, "Do not consider his appearance or his height, for I have rejected him." The Lord does not look at the things man looks at. Man looks at the outward appearance, but the Lord looks at the heart.' Can anyone tell me what this verse is all about?"

My hand shot up. "Yeah," I said with a satisfied smile. "It's about accepting others."

"Exactly," Mrs. Taylor replied.

I resisted the urge to look over at Simon and Simone. This was clearly a lesson we all needed to learn.

My feelings of satisfaction lasted through the entire service and the drive home. They evaporated when, after I'd changed into my Sunday loaf-around-the-house clothes, my mother cornered me in the kitchen and asked for Jackie Sue's phone number. Having no reason I could think of *not* to give it to her, I surrendered it. Then I hung around the kitchen to eavesdrop on her end of the conversation.

"Hello? Oh, hello, Jackie Sue, it's Mrs. Baker. Is your

mother available? Oh, no problem, I'll call back another time. Good—what? Oh yes, she's right here."

I leaped out of my chair, grabbed the phone, and looked over at my mother with my hand over the mouthpiece. My mother rolled her eyes and left the room.

"Hey, Jackie Sue," I said.

"Why is your mother calling here?" she snapped.

I didn't like her tone. "She wants to invite your mother to dinner. You know that."

"Well, that's a crappy idea, Tip," she said.

"So you've said. What would you like me to do about it?"

"Stop her."

She obviously didn't know my mother very well.

"She's got your number, Jackie Sue. What am I supposed to do, follow her around every minute of the day and keep her away from phones?"

Jackie Sue groaned. "Well, maybe if we stall her long enough she'll forget the whole thing."

"Maybe, but highly unlikely," I said. We were both quiet for a minute. "Would it be such a bad thing? I mean, it's only one dinner."

Jackie Sue didn't seem convinced. "I'll just keep answering the phone when I'm here and unplug it when I leave."

And Jackie Sue's plan worked. For about three weeks. Then the Monday before Thanksgiving, the two of us walked into my house to find my mother hanging up the phone.

"Good afternoon, ladies," she said.

"Hi, Mommy," I said suspiciously. "Why are you home so early? Something wrong?"

"Things are fine, dear. One of my clients canceled on me so I came home early. But I'm glad to see you, Jackie Sue," she continued, with a crafty smile. "I was just speaking with your mother. You two will be joining us for Thanksgiving dinner."

Jackie Sue and I stared at her, stunned.

"It's strange, Jackie Sue," my mother continued lightly. "Your mother had no idea I'd been trying to get in touch with her for the past three weeks."

"I . . . it's that . . . I'm a little disorganized," Jackie Sue said. "And I put all those messages on little bits of paper and stuff and I guess they all got misplaced."

"Of course," my mother said. "Well, that's water under the bridge now. We will see you here Thursday at four o'clock sharp."

"Great, Mrs. Baker," Jackie Sue said in a falsely cheery voice. "That's just great."

My mother left the room looking triumphant as Jackie Sue sank into a kitchen chair and put her head in her hands.

"Come on, Jackie Sue," I said, sitting beside her. "How bad could it possibly be?"

Jackie Sue looked at me and shook her head ominously.

16

Thanksgiving morning the skies were bright blue and everything was covered with the first blanket of snow. The view outside the window was blinding. With things so clean and fresh-looking I couldn't help feeling hopeful that everything would turn out all right. Dinner would go splendidly and Jackie Sue's mom wouldn't be nearly as awful as Jackie Sue had made her out to be.

The moment I stepped outside to get the morning paper with only my pajamas and slippers on it dawned on me that you couldn't always rely on appearances. The sun had fooled me. It was about five degrees out. Those few seconds outside created a cold feeling inside that I couldn't shake the rest of the day.

By three o'clock the sun gave up and clouds appeared. It started to get dark. My parents showered and changed into nicer clothes for dinner.

At a quarter till four my mother began setting out all the dishes of steaming hot food. At four o'clock sharp my father finished carving the turkey, and placed it in the center of our formal dining room table. The three of us stood back for a moment, admiring the setting and my mother's beautiful food. Normally this would be the time my father would say grace and we'd sit down to eat. But at 4:15 we were still fidgeting around, waiting for Jackie Sue and her mother to show up. At 4:30 my mother asked me, through slightly clenched teeth, to call her and see if perhaps they needed a ride over because of the snow that had started to fall.

I scurried to the phone and dialed Jackie Sue's number. It rang and rang and rang. No answer.

"They must be on their way," I said brightly. My father glared at my mother as 4:45 came and went, and along with it, his patience.

"Annie Lu," said my father, his voice full of irritation. I think he thought that if he used my mother's nickname it would somehow soften his tone of voice. It didn't. "I know you invited these people out of the kindness of your heart, but now, honey, the food is cold and I'm hungry, so I am going to say grace and eat."

Seconds after my father finished saying grace the doorbell rang. I ran to the door and yanked it open. Jackie Sue and her mother stood there, their arms filled with food.

"We didn't think you were coming!" I said as I let them in.

"Oh, chile, of course we were coming!" Jackie Sue's mother shouted. "Wouldn't miss it for the world." She shoved all the plates she was holding into my arms and grabbed me in a hug. "What a pleasure it is to finally meet you!"

Jackie Sue's mother was a thin blond wreck of a woman. If you looked closely you could see what remained of her pageant show beauty, but she smelled of sweat and alcohol and she was talking very loudly. I looked over her shoulder at Jackie Sue. She had the look of someone heading to the guillotine.

My parents appeared behind me.

"Um, Mom, Dad, this is Mrs. Webster," I stammered.

"Well, Mrs. Webster," my mother said, extending her hand, "I thought perhaps you had gotten a better offer."

"Well, ain't you just the prettiest gal," drawled Jackie Sue's mom, vigorously shaking my mother's hand. "You look just like that actress that plays the little colored nurse in the television show."

My mother's eyebrows shot up and my father lowered his head. Jackie Sue's face looked pinched.

Jackie Sue's mother must have mistaken our stunned silence for confusion. "Oh, come on, y'all. That show with the Negro nurse and her little son, cute little ole colored boy. Jackie Sue, you know the show I'm talking about."

"Diahann Carroll," I answered quietly. "In *Julia*." My mother and father turned and looked at me as if I'd gone crazy.

"Yes, that's right!" Jackie Sue's mother shouted, clapping me so hard on the back that I almost dropped the plates I was holding.

"Yes, well, that's very nice of you to say," my mother said stiffly. "Now, what do you have here? You really didn't have to bring a thing."

"I thought I'd give y'all a little taste of the south. We got some corn bread stuffing, sweet potato casserole, some homemade rolls, and a dump cake."

"Oh my, that's quite a lot of food," my mother said, leading the way back into the dining room.

"It was the least I could do, you being so kind as to invite my daughter and me to your lovely home here."

"Oh, it is our pleasure. Now, let's see. Mrs. Webster, you sit here. Morris, would you please?" my mother said, indicating that my father should hold the chair for Jackie Sue's mom. Jackie Sue took the seat next to her mother, and I sat across from them.

"My, y'all sure do have some pretty manners," Jackie Sue's mother said. "I do hope that some of them rub off on my daughter. She ain't got no kind of manners."

"I doubt that," my mother remarked as she took her seat. "I must say she has an impressive vocabulary."

Jackie Sue looked over at my mother and smiled gratefully.

"Well, I suppose. But them fancy words won't take her as far as good manners will. I've been trying to tell her that for years. Menfolk don't care how many big words you know."

"What can I get you to drink?" my father interrupted. He'd obviously had enough of our chitchat.

"Well, I think it would be a shame to put these here wineglasses to waste. Don't you?" Jackie Sue's mom said, handing her wineglass to my father. I heard Jackie Sue groan.

"Wine, then? Red or white?"

"Whichever is closest."

Jackie Sue leaned over to her mother and said, "Mom, why don't you have what everyone else is having? The sparkling apple cider?"

"Well, I would, sweetie, except Mr. Bunker here has already filled my glass with this nice red wine." She quickly took a large gulp of the wine, lowering the level of the glass by half.

"It's Baker, Mom, not Bunker," Jackie Sue told her.

"Well, who said it wasn't?"

There was an uncomfortable silence, until my father abruptly started dishing food onto his plate. I followed his lead and the next few minutes were quiet except for the sounds of forks hitting china, as we all served ourselves.

"So, Mrs. Webster," my mother said. "What exactly do you do? Jackie Sue says you're kept quite busy with your job. You work the night shift, right?"

I cringed and looked sidelong at Jackie Sue, who briefly met my eyes before concentrating on cutting her turkey into bite-size pieces.

"Oh, sweetie, it's not *Mrs.* Webster. It ain't *Mrs.* Anything. It's just plain ole Miss. Couldn't never find a man good enough to marry. And of course, it ain't so easy to get one when you got a child. Not too many want to raise someone else's left-behind, if you catch my meaning. So, you can just go ahead and call me Mae. Short for Maelinda Sue. That's where the Sue in Jackie Sue's name comes from."

Jackie Sue sank low in her chair and began mechanically feeding herself forkfuls of turkey.

My mother nodded slowly. "Yes, well, Jackie Sue seems quite . . . well adjusted. As I said earlier, I've always been impressed with her vocabulary. She's a smart young lady. You must be proud."

Mae shrugged her shoulders dismissively.

"Yeah, well, Jackie Sue has her uses, I'll grant her that. But fancy words ain't going to get her nowhere or no man. She's going to have to rely on her looks to get ahead in this world, just like I did." She punctuated this comment with a long swig of wine, gulping down the last of what was in her glass. My father, being a proper host, automatically refilled it. "You see, us white ladies don't really have to work for a living unless we want to. I was never a—what are they calling themselves these days? Feminists? Yeah, well, I ain't no feminist. I think the proper place for a true lady is in the home taking care of her family. Now I know you Blacks have to work, but a white lady should be a homemaker." Mae took another deep sip of her wine. "Which really is a shame, since Black women are so good at cooking and cleaning and such. I'm sure your husbands would love for you to use your housekeeping skills in your own homes."

My parents and I sat dumbfounded, while Mae downed her second glass of wine. She then held out her glass to my father, who refilled it again, much to Jackie Sue's dismay.

"Jesus, Mom!" she blurted out.

"Mind your manners, Jackie Sue! I was just saying, baby, that them feminists have it all wrong. With your looks you can find yourself a nice, rich boy who will take care of you."

My father couldn't stand it anymore. "Can I get anyone some more turkey?" he asked. "Potatoes? Green beans? Stuffing? Anything?"

"Tell me, Mr. Brinker," Mae slurred. "If you were a white man and could take care of your family without sending your wife out to work, wouldn't you want her at home?"

My father opened his mouth to respond, but my mother was faster.

"First of all, *Miss* Webster, it's Baker, not Brinker. Secondly, I work because I *choose* to work, not because my husband is incapable of supporting us. But perhaps we should change the subject, as it's clear that we have differing views on such matters."

Mae finished her glass of wine again. This time, she reached over, picked up the bottle, and filled her own glass. "That's probably a good idea," she said to my mother breezily. "Such subjects ain't proper for polite company."

For a moment all you could hear was the clinking of our eating utensils on my mother's best china. I could feel my mother radiating anger on one end of the table and my father seething on the other.

"Miss Webster, these sweet potatoes are delicious!" I blurted out. "It must have taken you all day long to cook this food. I've never had sweet potatoes like this before. We usually have regular mashed potatoes, but I really like these. I mean, they're mashed but, you know, sweeter than regular potatoes. I guess that's why they're called sweet potatoes."

I ran out of breath. Silence fell around the table again like a big musty blanket.

"Well, I don't know about anyone else, but I certainly am ready for dessert," my father announced. I surveyed the plates. My plate was still half-full, my mother's looked as if she had just started eating, and Mae's plate was untouched.

"Yeah, sounds great, Daddy," I said. I was still hungry, but game for anything that would make this night end more quickly. We hadn't been at the dinner table a half hour yet, but it felt like an eternity.

My mother got up from her chair. "I'll make coffee for us to drink with the dessert," she said pointedly. I noticed that Mae had downed the last of the wine in the bottle, and was staring bleary-eyed at the side table that sat against the wall behind me—the one with the row of wine and liquor on it. "Tiphanie," my mother continued, snatching my plate from under me, "help me clear the table please."

My father stood too, picking up his own plate. Then he followed my mother out of the dining room.

"May I take your plates?" I asked Jackie Sue and Mae. Jackie Sue nodded without looking up. Mae waved her hands at her dishes as if I was the waitress at a restaurant and it was time for me to clear the table. I picked up their plates and walked into the kitchen to find my parents hissing at each other while my mother attacked pies with a knife. They didn't seem to notice that I'd entered the room.

"Morris, I had no idea she was like that," my mother whispered as she slid one pie out of the way and began stabbing another.

My father was busy with the coffeemaker. "So, you're telling me that you had no idea what type of people Tiphanie has been associating with for the last few weeks?"

"You've seen that girl almost as often as I have," my mother hissed back, snatching the dump cake pan so she could attack that too. "Don't you dare blame this on me! Furthermore, that child in there is fine, it's the mother that's a drunken wreck."

"Apples don't fall too far from the tree," my father said, raising his voice. "And that drunk, white tra—"

"Daddy! Shh! They might hear you!" I whispered, cutting him off. "It's not that bad. I mean, she's not . . ." I trailed off.

My mother rolled her eyes at me. "Girl, please. That woman is a lush if ever I saw one."

"I don't like this type of influence at all," my father said. "Not at all."

"We should get back to our guests," I told them angrily. I turned tail and walked quickly back to the dining room.

Jackie Sue was fussing at her mother, who had helped herself to a bottle of wine from the side table and poured herself a generous glass. I sank into my chair.

My parents reappeared in the dining room carrying the desserts and three cups of coffee. They both stopped short when they saw the new wine bottle sitting on the table, but neither said anything.

Jackie Sue suddenly burst into tears.

"Now, sweetie," my mother coaxed. "You just try my apple pie. I'm famous for it." She slid a plate with a large piece in front of Jackie Sue. Jackie Sue tried to smile, but it didn't reach her eyes. But when she picked up her fork and put a small piece of pie in her mouth, a true smile flitted across her face.

"See?" my mother said, patting Jackie Sue on the back.

We all sat quietly, eating our dessert—all of us except Mae, who was ignoring the pie and the cup of coffee that had been set in front of her. She downed the rest of her wine and sat clutching the glass close to her chest as if afraid someone was going to take it from her.

I finished my apple pie and got up to get another piece. As I was serving myself, I heard a sharp intake of breath, a gasp, and then a snort. I turned around to find that Mae had passed out into her pie, her cheek resting on the smashed remains.

Thanksgiving dinner was officially over.

17

After Mae passed out, my father carried her to our car and laid her out on the backseat. Jackie Sue climbed into the front, sitting as still as stone, staring straight ahead. When my father returned fifteen minutes later, he disappeared into his study without a word.

The next morning I lingered in my room, reluctant to go downstairs. I was not in the mood for a "You need to be careful who you associate with" lecture, which I knew *must* be coming. Finally, after being called to the breakfast table for the third time, I marched into the kitchen ready for battle. But to my surprise, my parents acted as if nothing had happened the night before. I looked at them over my waffles, waiting. But there were no lectures, no speeches, nothing. I found it very suspicious, but I decided to leave well enough alone for the time being.

After my parents left for work I headed back up to my room and took a nice after-breakfast nap. When I woke, I called Jackie Sue. It took a while but she finally picked up.

"Hey, ready to do a little Christmas shopping?" I asked cheerfully. I was trying to keep up the charade of normalcy my parents had started that morning.

Unfortunately, stark reality was more Jackie Sue's style. "Do your parents know you're calling me?" she asked.

"I don't know. Sure, I guess. I mean, I assume they do. I call you every day."

"That was before my mother got drunk off your parents' wine and passed out in their cherry pie," she answered. "Not that I can blame your parents' wine for getting her drunk. She was more than halfway there before we even showed up. As usual."

In the background I heard Mae say something but I couldn't quite make it out.

"I'm not talking to you, Ma!" Jackie Sue snapped. Then she lowered her voice again. "So what you're saying is that they don't really know that you're calling me."

"They didn't tell me that I couldn't call you," I answered. "And by the way, it was apple pie, not cherry, that she passed out in."

Silence. I guess Jackie Sue wasn't ready to joke about that yet.

"Yeah, well, I don't really feel like hanging out today," she said finally.

"Come on, Jackie Sue, you can't spend the rest of the weekend stuck at home." I was concerned about her, but I was also itching to get out of the house. "How about a movie? My treat!"

"I don't need your charity," Jackie Sue said. "I've got enough money for a movie."

"Um, okay," I said. "So is that a yes then?"

"Yeah, whatever," Jackie Sue said. "I'll meet you at the corner in fifteen minutes. You know the one, where my wrong side of the tracks butts up against your right side."

She hung up before I could answer.

Fifteen minutes later we were sitting quietly at the bus stop together, watching the cars zoom by and squinting against the sunlight bouncing off the snow. I didn't know which felt colder, the ten-degree weather or Jackie Sue.

"Um, so, is your mom okay?" I asked.

Jackie Sue snorted. "Yeah, Tip, she's great. She's spending the day nursing her hangover with the proverbial hair of the dog. She should be nice and drunk again by the time I get home."

"Well, maybe you should . . ." I stopped abruptly, realizing that I had no idea what Jackie Sue should do.

She snorted again. "Thanks for the great advice. I'll do just that."

Luckily, at that moment the bus came.

The rest of the afternoon was awful. We saw *The Apple Dumpling Gang*, which had to be one of the dumbest movies ever made. After the movie we sat shivering in the cold, waiting for the bus to take us back home.

"Do you feel like getting some pizza?" I suggested.

"No."

"You sure? It will be my tre—" Jackie Sue glared at me, daring me to finish the sentence. I didn't. "Never mind," I muttered.

At last the bus appeared, crowded with holiday shoppers. Jackie Sue and I sat apart from each other, which was fine with me.

At our stop we got off and stood staring over each other's shoulders—both of us unwilling to look the other in the eye.

"Well," Jackie Sue mumbled, "bye."

"Thanks for a lovely and fun-filled afternoon," I said. "Your company was such a joy." Then I glanced at her and realized that she was crying. My anger disappeared. I put my arm around her. "Sorry," I said softly. "That was mean."

"No, you were justified in being that way," Jackie Sue said with a sniffle. "I know I've been a misanthrope all afternoon. Like my appalling life is your fault. I shouldn't be taking it out on you. You're my only friend. If I lose you I've got nothing."

"You aren't going to lose me!" I exclaimed.

She smiled an unhappy smile. "I saw the way your parents looked at my mother," she said. "I can imagine what they think of her. And of me."

"They didn't say anything to me about last night, or about you," I told her. She looked at me unbelievingly. "Honest, Jackie Sue, cross my heart."

"Really?" she said, swiping the tears off her face. "I was positive they'd forbid you to see me or something."

"No, I swear. They didn't say a thing. Not a single word."

Jackie Sue took a deep breath and let it out with a tremendous sigh of relief. "I just knew that our friendship was over. I was steeling myself for it all day. Like this was our last goodbye or something."

I laughed. "No way. First of all, I would never let our last goodbye be seeing a movie that lame. And second of all, we'll be friends until we are little ole ladies that are so hard of hearing we have to talk to each other with those ear megaphone thingies."

"They're called ear trumpets," Jackie Sue said, wiping the last of her tears away. For the first time all day, she looked like herself.

"How do you know stuff like that?" I asked.

She shrugged and grinned at me.

"So, you coming over or what?" I asked.

She suddenly looked tense again. "I don't know," she said, putting her hair in her mouth.

"We've got leftovers."

She smiled. "Well, maybe for a little while, but only until it's time for your parents to get home."

Usually I would have pooh-poohed that comment and convinced her to stay later. Maybe even spend the night. But this time I simply nodded, grabbed her arm, and led her in the direction of my house.

All in all, it was a pretty good ending to a crappy day.

For the rest of Thanksgiving break Jackie Sue and I pretended that nothing had happened. We hung out all day Saturday at the mall, and my parents never said a word, although they seemed to be spending a lot more time than normal in my dad's study. But the only unusual thing my mom said was, "Don't make plans for next weekend."

"Why?" I asked.

"Booker and Breeze Club," she said, which wasn't much of an answer.

"What?"

"We—well, actually you, since it's more of a youth group than anything else—have been invited to become members of Booker and Breeze and we—you—accepted."

"I have?" I whined. "I've never even heard of it. It sounds like something for babies."

"It's not. It's a great organization and only the very best Afro-American families are invited to join. You can't even ask for membership information. One of the members has to recommend you. It's really quite a privilege and an honor to be asked. And it couldn't have come at a better time."

I ignored that last comment. "But I won't know anyone. I'm tired of being the new person. Besides, it sounds like a bunch of snotty people. I mean, why haven't I been asked before? Why am I suddenly good enough now?"

"Your father wasn't a vice president at the bank before, and it's not exactly cheap to become a member," my mother told me. "Look, honey, it's a great opportunity. You'll like it, I promise. And it couldn't hurt for you to branch out a little in the friendship department. You know, just because we haven't talked about Thanksgiving doesn't mean we've forgotten about it. So, don't make any plans with Jackie Sue this coming weekend. You're busy."

Oh, so it was like that.

The Lay Down with Dogs Lecture

Tiphanie, your father and I don't understand why you choose to hang out only with Jackie Sue. Surely there must be other young ladies at school with whom you can socialize—young ladies from better circumstances. I'm not saying that Jackie Sue isn't a lovely girl. She's fine— incredible vocabulary. I just hope you haven't alienated the other girls.

Like my daddy used to say, "Lay down with dogs, get up with fleas." That holds true here just as much as it did in our old neighborhood.

18

The next Saturday morning my mother woke me up much earlier than I would have liked, and by nine o'clock we were driving into Denver.

"So what exactly is Booker and Breeze?" I asked her.

"It's an old, exclusive social and civic organization. You'll hear all about it once we get there. The mothers get together and work on political or community issues that will benefit the children, and the kids get together and learn something or play."

"Learn something or play," I said, rolling my eyes. "Sounds like preschool, Mom."

"Keep an open mind, Tiphanie," my mother said.

Like I had any other choice.

After a forty-minute drive we finally pulled into the driveway of a huge home set off of Meadow Hills Golf Course.

"Whoa!" I said, more to myself than to my mother.

"Yes, it's the Hunters' house."

"Who?"

"Trey Hunter, he's a Black man who owns a ton of real estate in town. Apartment buildings, office buildings, shopping complexes. Mostly in the Walnut Hill area and Five Points, but still, land is land."

She straightened her coat and hat before giving me a final appraising look. Then, with a deep breath, she rang the doorbell. An old Black woman in a maid outfit answered.

"Hello, we're here for the Booker and Breeze meeting," my mother told her demurely.

Once we were ushered inside, my mother was taken to the living room, where I caught a quick glimpse of my dentist's wife and a couple of the wealthier women from my church, drinking coffee and chatting quietly. I was led to the basement, which was unlike any basement I had ever seen. There was a huge console television against one wall and a stereo system lining another. A couple of pinball machines stood in the corner, along with Ping-Pong and foosball tables. Strangely, nobody in the room was playing any of these games. Instead, about a dozen kids close to my age were seated on the big sectional couch or on the floor. They seemed to be giving all their attention to the teenage boy standing at the stereo.

"Okay, so that was the horn section from 'Can't Hide Love.' It's complex and layered, so I think it can be part of our argument about our groups' talent with instruments. Now what about lyrics?"

The group sank immediately into deep thought. I had no

idea what was going on. I walked over to the nearest girl and whispered, "What are you guys doing?"

She looked up at me. "Well, Teddy—he's the one at the stereo—he got into this discussion with his father about music. You know, the same old jive, 'You young people don't know good music. Your generation's music is awful.' Well, then his brother, Big Mouth James over there, says he can easily prove that our music is as good as what they listened to at our age."

"Um, Charlene, I can hear you, you know," Big Mouth James called over to us. "Hi, new girl. What's your name?"

"It's Tiphanie," I said, smiling at him.

Charlene leaned over and poked the guy who was sitting next to her in the shoulder. "Marcus, umm, what was our original plan for today's B&B meeting?" she asked, rolling her eyes.

Marcus chuckled before answering, "Game day."

"And why exactly are we *not* playing games right now?" she asked him.

"Well, because we are working on a list of songs to compare and contrast to make the point that our music is on par with or exceeds the quality of the music of our parents' generation."

"And who is responsible for giving us this extra research project?" Charlene asked.

"I would have to say it is the fault of Big Mouth James Hunter over there," Marcus said, pointing an accusatory finger at James.

Over the laughter of the group, James whined, "Come on, man! You're supposed to have my back."

"Hey, everyone," Charlene said. "This is Tiphanie, our new girl. Tiphanie, this is everyone. You'll eventually figure out names, but right now we're in a hurry." She shot an evil look at James. "Trying to salvage our game day."

"Does this research project have to be done today?" I asked.

"Well, Big Mouth James," answered another guy sitting across from James, "told his old man that we could prove it to him before the end of our meeting today. Hi, I'm Clark Prentiss, Tiphanie, nice to meet you."

"Not only that," piped up a girl sitting on the floor in front of Clark. "Mr. Hunter took the paddles, the board games, and all the other stuff, so we could focus on our research and not be distracted by the games. Yvette Willis, a pleasure."

"So basically, Big Mouth James messed up our whole meeting today," finished Marcus.

"Yes," Yvette interjected, "because of Big Mouth James we are stuck trying to find songs from the, um . . . Hey, what years are we talking about here anyway?"

"The 1950s?" Big Mouth James said uncertainly.

"Nah, too much good music from then," Clark answered. "Besides, our parents are what? Forty years old or so?"

"You could use that old record 'Ting-A-Ling,' " I suggested. "Or Little Richard's 'Rice, Red Beans and Turnip Greens.' Then compare those lyrics to some Jackson Five songs. Like, say, 'Looking Through the Windows.' The words to that are pretty deep."

"Oh, that's good," said Marcus. "My mom and dad love Little Richard."

An hour later, I felt more at home with these kids than I'd felt in a long time. After a successful music presentation where we more than proved our point to our parents, we spent the rest of the afternoon playing games and talking. It turned out half of the Booker and Breeze kids lived in areas where they were one of the few Blacks at their schools too. After hearing some real horror stories, I started to feel better about my life.

"Shoot, my sister and I had to run home every day in elementary school," Clark said with a laugh. "Them crackers thought it was funny to throw rocks and stuff at us. Every day! They never got tired of it."

"What is it with them and throwing stuff?" Charlene said. "I started skipping lunch when I went to Evergreen Junior High. They were forever throwing food at me. I got tired of washing fruit cocktail out of my hair."

"Well, at least they kept their distance from you," James said.

"Yeah, James and I had to fight just about every day while we were waiting for the bus," Teddy added. "Of course, that only lasted the first week of school. They finally figured out that if they called us that word every day, then they'd get a beat-down every day."

"I didn't have to deal with all that," said Yvette. "But it

can sure get lonely doing everything by yourself all the time. Those white folk pretend I don't even exist."

On the way home it occurred to me that going to that Booker and Breeze meeting had had the opposite effect on me than my parents had hoped. Rather than drive me further away from Jackie Sue, listening to the other kids' stories had made me realize how lucky I was to have her—and it made me more determined to be a better friend to her than ever before.

19

On Monday, Jackie Sue arrived at school wearing an ultra-short miniskirt—a first for her.

"Hey," I said. "What's with the skirt?"

"Just going for a change," she said. "Sometimes you just want to be someone else for a while, you know?"

"But don't you think it's a little, uh, short?" I said as she rummaged through her locker.

"It's just a skirt, Tip," she said. "It's not that big a deal." She slammed her locker shut. "See you at lunch."

After school I was bundling up for the walk home when Jackie Sue came rushing up to my locker.

"Come on, let's go," she said.

"Okay, let me get my scarf on. It's so cold out," I whined. She must have been freezing in that skirt, but she wasn't letting on. "Why does winter always seem to last so long?"

"It's not winter yet, it's still autumn. Winter doesn't officially start until December 22. Come on, put your scarf on outside. Let's go." I followed her gaze down the length of the hallway and saw Clay and Grant rounding the corner. I grabbed my things, kicked my locker closed, and hurried over to the front doors.

"Hey!" someone shouted from behind us.

Jackie Sue's pace quickened. "Walk faster," she said.

"Yo! Wait up!" the voice called. Suddenly it dawned on me that the voice didn't belong to Clay. I glanced behind me to see Bradley jogging up to us. Clay and Grant were farther behind him.

"Dang," Bradley said once he'd caught up to us. "What's the rush?"

"We aren't in the mood to deal with Clay and Grant, that's all," I answered.

Bradley rolled his eyes. "They don't have any power over you guys. Relax. You can't let them push you around. When you do that you give them the upper hand."

He slowed down and started to walk at a normal speed. We matched his pace, but Jackie Sue looked over her shoulder several times. Her face was like stone. I wondered what Clay would say to her now that she was walking with both me *and* Bradley. I felt like I was making Jackie Sue choose between my friendship and having a home. But since I couldn't tell Bradley what the deal was, and Jackie Sue wasn't going to say anything, what was I supposed to do?

"So, are you guys going on the ski trip weekend after next?" Bradley asked.

I laughed. "You know we Black people don't ski," I said.

"I don't know about *you* Black people, but *me* Black people skis. And very well by the way, in case you were wondering. I'm all, whoosh, whoosh, whoosh." He mimicked ski-ing, adding a little extra dip for soul.

"I don't know, I've never been before," I said.

"I can teach you guys," Bradley offered. "Come on, I'll be your official mountain host."

"Well, I'll try anything once," I told him. "But I'll have to ask my mom. She's suddenly my social planner. She's got me signed up for Booker and Breeze."

"Booker and Breeze, really?" he said, coming to a stop as we arrived at his block. He sounded impressed. "My mom's been trying to get us invited for years."

"Well, I'll tell my mom to call your mom. It'd be nice to know someone. I mean, the other kids are cool, but they've been together for a while. I'm tired of being the new per-son."

Bradley nodded, but he was watching Jackie Sue, who was watching Clay and Grant. They were closer now.

"It's really cold out," Jackie Sue said suddenly. "Let's hurry so we can get warm."

"Okay, well, see you guys tomorrow," Bradley said. Jackie Sue nodded and took off walking. Bradley looked at me with a raised eyebrow.

"It's a long story," I said. "See ya, Bradley."

"Yeah, I bet. Later, Tip."

I had to jog a little to catch up to Jackie Sue. Neither of us looked back.

Once Jackie Sue and I were safely at my house, our after-noon felt almost normal. We were in the kitchen replenishing our snacks when my mother came home from work. I suddenly felt tension in the air. It was the first time my mom and Jackie Sue had seen each other since the Thanksgiving fiasco.

"Hi, Mrs. Baker," Jackie Sue said quietly. She was looking at my mom like a puppy begging for a belly scratch.

"You going for a new look, Jackie Sue?" my mother asked. I flinched at the hardness in her tone. I'd gotten used to Jackie Sue's short skirt, but obviously it didn't sit well with my mother.

Jackie Sue seemed puzzled for a moment before reaching down to smooth out her skirt. "I thought I'd try something different," she replied stiffly.

My mother tilted her head to the side. "Well, I don't believe it suits you." Then her voice softened. "You're a pretty girl, you know. You don't need to dress like that. It distracts from your God-given beauty."

The defiance on Jackie Sue's face was replaced by surprise. "Yes, ma'am," she answered. She picked up her plate of food and left the kitchen.

My mother turned and narrowed her eyes at me. "I suggest that you don't try that look either, Tiphanie," she said curtly.

"Gosh, Mom, I know," I answered. I grabbed my plate and fled the kitchen.

In the den Jackie Sue was packing up her things. Tear tracks had made wet streaks down her cheeks.

"Don't go, Jackie Sue," I said, watching her stuff the snacks into her bag along with her homework.

"Did you see the way she looked at me?" Jackie Sue sniffed. She wiped at her tears.

"It was the skirt. It threw her a little."

"She looked at me like I was trash, Tip. Like I was nothing. She's never looked at me that way before! I don't know why I thought a new outfit could change my life. I shouldn't have come over here."

"No, Jackie Sue," I started, but she cut me off.

"It's my mother, isn't it? She doesn't want you hanging around with the daughter of a drunk, does she?"

"She hasn't said anything like that."

Jackie Sue snatched her bag up and headed to the door. "Yeah, well, she didn't have to." Then she looked at me, her eyes red, and said, "At Thanksgiving your mom told me I was smart."

I nodded.

"Bye, Tiphanie, see ya later," she said softly. She turned and walked out the front door. I closed it quietly behind her.

When I asked my mom about the ski trip, I was fully expecting her to turn me down. After all, I'd need money for the bus, the lift ticket, and the rental skis, not to mention something new to wear. My wool coat and knit mittens weren't going to do the trick. So I was stunned when she said yes—not only without protest, but happily.

"No problem, honey," she said excitedly. "This is great. You do know that Booker and Breeze take regular ski trips."

"I know, Mom," I answered. "I heard the kids talking about it at the last event."

"Now, you said it was Bradley Jepperson who suggested you go? His father's Floyd Jepperson, the former basketball player, right?"

"Yeah, I guess so." The guys in science were always talking about Bradley's father and basketball, but those were the times I zoned out. I wasn't much of a sports fan.

"He owns a very successful mortgage broker business," my mother gushed. "I'd love to meet him and see if maybe we could partner together on some real estate deals." I zoned out on her too, thinking about my Christmas vacation schedule. Between the Booker and Breeze events and all the church activities my mother had signed me up for, and now this ski trip, there wasn't going to be very much time to hang out with Jackie Sue.

"I'd thought perhaps they would take the first steps," my mother continued. "I mean, that would have been the polite thing to do, but there's no reason why we can't at least invite them to our New Year's Eve get-together. What do you think?"

"Huh?" I said. I'd tuned back in too late to have any idea what she was talking about.

"Oh, Tiphanie, stop daydreaming," she snapped. "I said why don't you invite Bradley and his family to our New Year's Eve get-together?"

"Um, I don't know, Mom."

"It's the perfect chance for you to broaden your social circle. Actually, what would you think of having a separate New Year's Eve party, just for you? You could invite Bradley and some of your new friends from Booker and Breeze, as well as the kids from church? You can have the den to hang out in. We'll move your stereo down there so you can dance."

I could see the wheels in my mother's head turning like crazy, and I was getting excited myself. I hadn't had a party since we'd moved out here.

"Ooohhh, can Jackie Sue spend the night?" I asked. "She can help me set up and get the food ready and stuff!"

My mother looked at me with a frown. "Tiphanie, honey, I don't think she'd feel comfortable at this type of party. She wouldn't know anyone at all. You haven't talked to Renee in ages. You could invite her."

"Renee and I, we just don't vibe anymore. Jackie Sue's my best friend now. And she'd be comfortable. She'd know *me*," I answered quietly, but I knew I'd lost this battle already. "And Bradley. She knows him."

"How about we have her spend the night on the second or the third of January, before school starts up again?"

"Please, Mom, let me invite her."

"No, it's for the best really. I'd hate for her to feel uncomfortable. Now, come on. We've got some ski shopping to do."

I sighed and got my coat.

By the end of the shopping spree I was more enthusiastic about the ski trip. I mean, what could be so hard about strapping long wooden planks to my feet and sliding down a mountain? Especially when I had a cute outfit on. I was still worried about not being able to invite Jackie Sue to my New Year's Eve party, but then again, what she didn't know couldn't hurt her, right?

20

The Saturday of the ski trip, my mother dropped me off at the school parking lot at 6:15 a.m. I walked over to the line of kids waiting to get on the school bus. It was hard to distinguish who was who underneath the hats and scarves, but I didn't see Bradley's dark brown face in the sea of pink and peach ones. I prayed he hadn't stood me up. I also hoped that Grant and Clay weren't skiers.

When I climbed onto the bus, I saw right away that the Barbies were there, and most of the jocks. There were a few random geeks as well. I finally spotted Bradley in the back, sitting next to Todd. I wanted to cry with relief. Denise was sitting by the window in the seat right in front of them, and the space next to her was empty. She smiled and waved me over.

"Hey, Tip, I didn't know you skied!" she said.

"I don't," I admitted. "Bradley talked me into coming. He claims he can teach me in one morning."

"Is that so, Bradley?" Denise said. "You think you can teach someone to ski before lunch?"

"Damn skippy!" Bradley hooted. Denise laughed and shook her head. Todd grinned at me.

"I think you'd better stick with me today," Denise said, turning back to me. "I've seen Bradley ski."

"Sounds good," I said. "Where's Gretchen?" Denise and Gretchen were usually inseparable.

"She's heading to Hawaii with her family. They have a house in Maui."

"Whoa," I said. "Is it nice?"

"As far as I can tell from the pictures, it is. My parents won't let me go. Every time I ask, they launch into a lecture about how conspicuous displays of wealth are part of the bourgeois establishment designed to keep the poor down-trodden." She sighed. "My parents used to be hippies. I was actually born on a commune."

I laughed. "You were born on a commune, but your name is Denise?"

"To be honest Denise is my middle name. My first name is Lovelystar."

"No way!"

"I'm afraid so," she said with a grimace. I burst out laughing.

By the time we arrived at the ski resort almost two hours later, I'd been laughing so hard my cheeks hurt.

The afternoon was a blast. Denise turned out to be a much better teacher than Bradley, although he did try. ("All ya gotta do is squat a little and then kind of push out to go and then turn your feet to stop. Get it?") By the end of the day I was skiing green runs with relative ease. When we got back to the school parking lot Denise and I exchanged phone numbers just as her parents came driving up in a beat-up, hand-painted Volkswagen bus. When my mother arrived, I introduced her to Bradley, and she told him to invite his parents to our New Year's Eve party.

That night, I stumbled to bed much earlier than usual. Only when I was drifting off to sleep did I stop to think about Jackie Sue and wonder what she'd done all day. But before I could feel guilty for forgetting to call her when I got home, I fell asleep.

The days before Christmas went by in a blur of activity. Between the Christmas pageant rehearsals at church and Booker and Breeze events and getting ready for my New Year's party, my days and nights were full to the brim with activities. I was so busy that I didn't stop to phone Jackie Sue until Christmas Eve.

"Ho! Ho! Ho!" I said merrily when she answered the phone.

"Hi, Tiphanie," she answered dryly. "Haven't heard from you lately."

"Yeah, I don't have much time right now either. I just got home from singing carols at an old folks' home with Booker and Breeze. I've got a couple hours before I have to go to church for the nativity play, so thought I'd check to see if you were home."

"Of course I'm home, Tiphanie," Jackie Sue answered. "I don't have a satiated and jubilant life like yours, remember?"

"Oh," I said, stunned at how quickly talking with Jackie Sue had made my warm holiday feelings fade. "Well, I just wanted to come by and bring you your Christmas gift."

The silence on the other end of the phone was so deep I began to think she'd hung up on me.

"Jackie Sue?" I asked. "You still there?"

"Yes, but you know, I didn't, I couldn't, get you any-thing," she answered. Her voice was soft, all the sarcasm gone.

"It's not about the getting," I said. "It's about the giving."

"Yeah, okay," she said. "Fine. Come by. Clay and his dad aren't around today, so I guess it's okay. My trailer's the last one, in the back."

"Great!" I said. "I'll be there in a little bit."

After she hung up, I stood there holding the phone for a moment, trying to relax. A part of me wished I could go over to Jackie Sue's another day. My house was decked out like a Black Norman Rockwell Christmas painting and I knew her trailer couldn't be half as warm and inviting. We had a big pine tree in the picture window of our living room loaded with candy canes, lights, and ornaments, and there were dozens of presents underneath. Lights and garlands were draped on the staircase and around the windows, and a fire crackled in the fireplace. In the kitchen, my mother was singing along—badly—to Nat King Cole's Christmas carols, but the heavenly smells drifting into the living room made up for it.

All I wanted to do was curl up in the big easy chair by the fire with a book and some cocoa until it was time to leave for the nativity play. I had a strong urge to call Jackie Sue back and tell her I couldn't come over after all. But just thinking that thought made me feel guilty. So after finally convincing my mom that I'd only be at Jackie Sue's for an hour, I put on my coat, gloves, scarf, and hat, grabbed her bag of presents, and headed outside.

It had been snowing off and on most of the day and there was a light, fluffy layer that made my neighborhood look festive and beautiful in the fading afternoon light. I walked slowly, enjoying the decorated houses and Christmas trees, but when I crossed Sheridan Boulevard things changed. Tacky plastic Santas leaned awkwardly on the lawns, and the few wreaths on the doors looked lonely and out of place. Even the snow was muddy and brown, marred by footprints and tire marks.

Walking past the first trailer, the one marked with the manager sign, I fought the urge to hide my face. I didn't want to cause any more trouble for Jackie Sue, but I knew I had a right to walk anywhere I wanted to with my head held high. My parents had worked hard for that. I concentrated on putting one foot in front of the other, walking as confidently as I could.

Jackie Sue's trailer sat haphazardly in the very last row, as though someone had gotten tired of driving it and had stopped and unhooked it in a rush. There was an old coffee can sitting by the door, filled with an incredible number of cigarette butts, and the screen door was missing its top half. I reached up to knock, but stopped when I heard yelling inside.

"You have got to be out of your cotton-pickin' mind!"

Mae was shouting, her words slurred. "You know you can't invite that gal over here! You wanna get us throwed out?"

"Mom, Clay and his dad aren't even home," Jackie Sue said back. "So just drop it."

"You aren't in charge here, missy, I am. And I say she doesn't come over!"

"Oh, please, Momma! You're in charge?" Jackie Sue's voice was dripping with scorn. "The only thing in your life you can control is the hand with the bottle in it."

"Watch your mouth, little girl. You show me respect! I could have been Miss America or Miss USA if it hadn't been for you, but noooo. Having you ruined my life, and I'm not going to live on the street just because you think you're special. So you call that colored gal right now and tell her she can't come!"

"No!" Jackie Sue screamed back. "I hate you! If you weren't so useless and drunk all the time—"

Just then I heard something that sounded very much like a slap, and suddenly the door was yanked open. Jackie Sue, her face wet with tears, came storming out. She bumped into me on their tiny front stoop, my gift in one hand and the other still raised in a fist to knock.

"Um, Merry Christmas?" I said. Jackie Sue closed her eyes, trying to compose herself.

"Jackie Sue!" Mae screamed from inside. "You get your tail back in here now!"

Jackie Sue reached behind and slammed the door shut. "I have to get out of here," she said. She brushed past me and hurried down the stairs.

"Jackie Sue! Hey!" I called, trotting after her. She was practically running, and her legs were much longer than mine. "Wait up! Where are you going?"

"I don't know," she said. "The park, maybe. It doesn't matter."

"The park? But it's so cold. Come with me! You could see me in the play. I'm the Herald Angel."

"Thanks, but I need to be by myself for a while. I have to think."

We got to the corner light in record time, and Jackie Sue punched the walk button furiously.

"But it's so cold," I said again.

"And?" she snapped.

"Well . . . here." I shoved the gift bag at her.

"I'm really not in the mood for presents," she said. "But I appreciate your munificence."

"My what?" I said.

Jackie Sue smiled softly. "Generosity, Tip. It means generosity."

"Well then, why can't you say that, you little show-off? Here." I dug through the bag until I found the packages I had carefully wrapped the night before.

"Just open them," I said. "Please."

Jackie Sue sighed, but she walked over to the nearby bus bench, sat down, and began to unwrap the gifts methodically, careful not to rip the paper.

"At this rate we'll both freeze to death," I said.

I reached over to help her with the wrapping paper, but she slapped my hand away. "Only people who get a lot of presents rip off the paper in a hurry," she told me. "Those of us who rarely receive gifts like to savor the experience. Okay?"

"Oh," I replied. I leaned back. "Take your time."

I'd given her an emerald green hat and scarf with gloves to match. They were thick and soft and warm. Jackie Sue pulled them out one by one, almost reverently, and laid them on her lap. Then she picked up the hat and rubbed it against her cheek. She closed her eyes and when she opened them again I could see teardrops glistening on her lashes.

"I thought the color would look great with your eyes," I said. "And they looked warm, and cozy too, and I thought, well, that's something you need. Something warm and cozy."

Jackie Sue nodded. She pulled the hat on, wrapped the scarf around her neck, and tugged on the matching gloves.

I looked at her with a smile. "That color makes your eyes sparkle." I said. Or maybe it was the tears that made them glimmer in the evening gloom.

Jackie Sue leaned over and gave me a slow, tight hug. "Thank you, Tiphanie," she whispered. "For everything." Then she stood, picked up the bag, and began to walk off.

"Merry Christmas!" I called to her. I didn't know whether she heard me or not. She never turned around. Maybe I should have chased after her, demanding that she come back to my house and not go wandering off somewhere in the cold, in the dark. But instead I sat on the bench in the growing twilight and watched her walk away, until I couldn't see her anymore.

21

Christmas came and went quietly. The scene on Christmas Eve with Jackie Sue had dampened my enthusiasm for the rest of the holiday. I couldn't shake the sad feeling I'd gotten watching her walk away. But every time I tried to call, Mae said she wasn't there.

"I'll tell her you rang," Mae said thickly the fifth time she answered the phone.

"Thank you, but when will she be back?"

"How the hell would I know?" Mae answered.

I hung up without another word.

For the next four days I called as often as I could. Mae was the only one who ever answered, and she never knew—or seemed to care—where Jackie Sue was. It was like my best friend had evaporated into thin air.

"What's the matter, honey?" my mother asked after I hung up the phone for what seemed like the fiftieth time on New Year's Eve. My face must have looked shocked.

"It's . . ." I started. Then I remembered the promise I'd made to Jackie Sue two months before. I wanted to tell my mother that Jackie Sue had disappeared, that something must be wrong, that she needed help. But in my head I heard Jackie Sue's voice telling me that she wasn't a charity case. "It's nothing."

Even with the worries about Jackie Sue floating around my head, I was still excited about my party that night. In all, I'd invited twenty-four friends—evenly split between boys and girls. Regina was the first to arrive, and together we greeted my other friends and escorted them downstairs to the den. An hour later, the party was in full swing. My friends were all getting along, talking and dancing, and I was having more fun than I could remember—when over the din of music and talking I heard a shriek.

Yvette was standing with a small group of kids, pointing out one of the basement windows.

"What's wrong?" I asked, hurrying over. "Are you okay?"

"A face!" Yvette shouted. "I swear I just saw a face looking in."

"What?" I said, peering out the window.

"Like a ghost," Yvette said. "I swear I saw a ghost peeking in."

"Dang, Tip," Joseph said. "Is that how it is in the 'burbs? You got white people keeping tabs on you and stuff? Is that what I have to look forward to in Aurora?"

I looked back out the window, a knot in my stomach. Suddenly Jackie Sue's face appeared. But the minute she saw me looking back at her, her face disappeared.

"Excuse me, everyone," I said. "I'll be right back." I ran up the basement stairs two at a time and yanked open the back door.

"Jackie Sue?" I called out. I trotted around to the front of the house and saw her walking quickly up the block. I ran to catch up, grabbing her arm to stop her. "Jackie Sue, wait! Where have you been? I've been trying to reach you forever!"

"And yet you still had time to plan a party," she said. "Amazing."

"Yeah, well, maybe you would have been invited if I'd been able to get in touch with you!" I said. Was that true? I wondered. Would I really have defied my mother and invited Jackie Sue? I wasn't quite sure.

"Doesn't matter, I've been very busy myself. In fact, I'm much in demand. I have to go."

She turned to leave, but I grabbed her arm again. "Wait, Jackie Sue," I said. She snatched her arm away but didn't walk off. What was she doing out so late anyway? And why hadn't she returned any of my phone calls? "Come to the party. We've got food and we're dancing and stuff. It's cold out here."

She shrugged, so I tugged her toward the house. It wasn't until we got to the light of my back porch that I got a good look at her. She was a mess. Underneath her new green hat her hair was stringy, dirty, and uncombed. Her coat was grimy and her jeans were filthy. She didn't smell all that great either. "I'll take you upstairs first," I said. "So you can, um, freshen up."

I led Jackie Sue quietly into the kitchen. Luckily, my

mother had her head deep in the oven, pulling out her famous stuffed mushrooms, and didn't notice us. I knew she'd kill me for bringing Jackie Sue to her fancy party, especially given the state Jackie Sue was in at the moment. But clearly something strange was going on with my best friend, and I didn't know what else to do.

Unfortunately, the only way upstairs to my room was right through my parents' party in the living room. And it seemed that the time for holiday miracles was over, because as soon as we stepped through the swinging door my mother came right behind us carrying the appetizer tray and announced merrily, "Come get them while they're hot!" Everyone in the living room turned to look our way.

I knew what they saw. Me in my black party dress, hair perfectly coiffed, pulling a dirty-faced, stringy-haired white girl in a ratty coat behind me.

There was an uncomfortably long silence, until the adults rearranged their faces, regained their manners, and turned back to chatting and laughing with each other as if they hadn't seen anything out of the ordinary. I hurriedly pulled Jackie Sue toward the stairs, not daring to look behind me. I could feel my mother's red-hot fury boring into the back of my head.

"A bath will warm you up," I told Jackie Sue once we made it to my room. I glanced at the door, expecting my mother to come barging in at any moment, but she seemed to have decided not to follow me.

"I'd like that," Jackie Sue said, sinking onto my bed.

I left to run the water, dumping in a lot of bubble bath. I

called her in once the tub was full, and she submerged herself in the water.

I tossed her a washcloth. "You have a smudge under your eye," I told her.

Jackie Sue wiped her face with the cloth, but the greenish hue around her eye didn't go away.

"You're missing it," I said. "It is right there." I poked the green spot and she grimaced.

The spot wasn't dirt, but the remains of a black eye.

"Oh no, Jackie Sue, what happened?" I asked.

She shook her head, looked down, and began to play with the bubbles.

"Jackie Sue?"

"It was an accident," Jackie Sue muttered. "It's not a big deal. It's just a bump. She was really drunk and didn't know what she was doing. She tends to get a little pugilistic when she drinks. I mean, she's slapped me before, but she's never . . . She wasn't really thinking clearly. She was angry with me and . . . we have to move out of the trailer park, and she's upset, that's all. Clay's dad told us last week. Tomorrow's our last day. Anyway, long story short, this bruise is what I got from my mother for Christmas."

I looked down at my hands, trying to think of something to say.

22

The next morning I awoke to the sound of knocking on my door. My mother entered the room. "Jackie Sue, would you please come downstairs with me?" she said.

Jackie Sue rubbed the sleep from her eyes and nodded. Pulling my robe over the pajamas I'd lent her the night before, she followed my mother downstairs. I trailed after them. Standing in our front doorway was a white woman I'd never seen before.

"Jackie Sue," my mother said, gently pushing her forward toward the woman. "This is Mrs. Green from the Arapahoe County Social Services. She's here to help you."

"I don't need help," Jackie Sue snapped. "I have a mother. I don't need any social services assistance."

"Judging by that black eye, you certainly do," Mrs. Green answered. There wasn't a trace of warmth in her voice. "After Mrs. Baker's phone call last night I took a preliminary visit to your home. Your mother was extremely inebriated and had no idea where you were when asked. We've taken her in so she can dry out. She'll probably be in detox for a few days. The Arapahoe County believes it's in your best interest to live elsewhere for a while."

"I can't leave my mother," Jackie Sue said. Her voice was quavering, her defiance gone. "She needs me. She won't even remember to eat if I'm not there."

"Now don't you worry about her," Mrs. Green said. "The place we've sent her will help her get better. Right now we're concerned with finding a good home for you."

"Can't I stay here?" Jackie Sue asked. She turned and looked at me, then at my mother.

Mrs. Green answered before either of us could. "There are official places we must put you, dear. The Bakers have a lovely home, but they wouldn't have called us if they hadn't seen the need for our help in placing you in an appropriate setting."

"Well, actually, Mrs. Green," my mother began, "I intended on requesting that you allow Jackie Sue to live with us temporarily. I believe I stated that to the person I spoke with on the phone. We have the room and it's really—"

"Yes, well, be that as it may," Mrs. Green interrupted, "that was before we saw that you were in no way related to her. As I have said, we have places that are better equipped to fill her cultural needs."

"My daughter and Jackie Sue are quite close," my mother said. "I would think it would be in her best interest to be somewhere she would be comfortable while things with her mother are being worked out."

"Yes, well, I appreciate your thoughts," Mrs. Green replied. "But seeing as you are clearly not a relative of Jackie Sue's, she is no longer your concern. Jackie Sue is now officially a ward of the court, and it is the court who will decide where she will be most comfortable."

"I'm so sorry, Jackie Sue," I whispered to her. But when she turned to face me, the look she gave me felt like a stab to the heart.

"Do get your things now, Jackie Sue. We must be going."

"I don't have any things," Jackie Sue said, yanking off my robe and reaching for the door.

After Jackie Sue and Mrs. Green walked outside, my mother closed the door softly.

"Why did you call them, Mommy?" I asked.

"It was the best thing to do, Tiphanie. I heard what was going on in your room last night. I know her mother hit her. You're a good friend, but you can't solve all her problems. Friendship can't solve everything."

"But I should have at least tried, Mom."

January 1976

The Keep Up the Good Work Lecture

Your mother and I are proud of you, Tiphanie. Don't think we don't know how hard the situation we placed you in has been. Even if you'd gone to a school with more Afro-Americans, being the new kid would have been tough. But you put your nose to the grindstone and worked hard.

We know that we expect a lot from you. But it's nothing you can't do. You're older now, and being older not only comes with a great deal of privileges, it also comes with responsibility. You've matured quite a bit in the past few months. Things usually turn out for the best, even if at first that doesn't seem to be the case.

23

School started the next week with the usual confusion that came from beginning all new classes. Between each class period I scanned the halls, looking desperately for Jackie Sue, but I didn't see her anywhere. She wasn't in any of my new classes either. At lunch I walked to the cafeteria, steeling myself to eat alone. But Denise came up to me the minute I stepped foot into the lunchroom.

"Oh, thank God, Tip! I don't know anyone. Please, please, please can we eat together?" She grabbed my arm. "Don't leave me in here all alone! I can't take it. I've a delicate constitution."

I laughed. I really did like Denise quite a bit. "I'm glad you're here too," I said.

It turned out Bradley and Steve also had lunch that period, and the four of us spent the hour laughing more than eating.

Jackie Sue didn't appear at school that whole week. I

called every day when I got home, but the telephone always rang without ever being answered.

When Saturday arrived, I got up early and walked over to the trailer park. I didn't know if Mae was out of detox yet, or if Clay's dad had kicked her out of the trailer for good, but I was determined to find her so I could figure out exactly where Jackie Sue was, and I had nowhere else to look. It had snowed during the night, and when I got to their trailer I saw a dozen little snow-covered hills out front. As I got closer I realized that the heaps of snow were actually boxes of clothes, kitchen utensils, and trophies. I was about to knock on the door when I noticed a shiny padlock on the screen.

"I told them they weren't going to be living here much longer if they didn't listen to me."

I turned and saw Clay, standing there with a smirk on his face. "Had to kick your friend's trampy mother out." He shoved one of the boxes with his stupid moonboots, knocking the snow off a pile of clothes. "Freeloaders."

I stood on the tiny porch and stared down at him angrily. "Where's Jackie Sue?" I asked.

"Don't know. Don't care either. I had to dig all their crap out of the trailer on Friday. Took me all afternoon. Never saw so many empty bottles of booze in my life. It was worth it, though. We can't keep letting losers live here. Especially ones who don't pay the rent. Not to mention the riffraff they invite over."

"Seems to me that if you don't want any losers around

here then you and your dad need to move out too," I said. I charged down the stairs to confront him.

"Shut up," Clay snapped. He took a step toward me. I turned to get away, but fell over one of the boxes.

Clay laughed. "Your friend was a tramp and her mother was a drunk," he said, watching me try and get back on my feet.

"Up yours, Clay," I said.

"Get off our property. Your kind isn't welcome here." With that, he turned and walked away.

I brushed the dirt and snow off myself and I looked through the box that I'd fallen over. Underneath the trophies, crowns, and water-soaked sashes was a framed picture. I picked it up.

A beautiful, young, fresh-looking Mae was sitting on a tire swing somewhere in the country, holding Jackie Sue as a toddler. Jackie Sue's face was snuggled into her mother's neck, and her green eyes were sparkling. Mae looked as if she was caught mid-laugh—her eyes clear and happy. It was a gorgeous picture.

Right then I understood why, despite everything, Jackie Sue had always been so fiercely loyal to her mother. Once, sometime ago, they'd gotten it right. It was to *those* memories that Jackie Sue had clung so stubbornly all these years.

I laid the photograph down gently on top of the trophies and picked up the box. Then I carried it home. I returned four more times to the trailer park, ignoring the shouts from Clay's trailer each time I walked by. I left the clothes, the shoes, the pots and pans. The boxes I carried home were the things I thought Jackie Sue would want—the photos, a worn dictionary, and the things from her bedroom. I stashed them behind the Christmas decorations in our garage, taking only the picture of Mae and Jackie Sue on the swing into the house with me. That I kept on my nightstand, next to my favorite picture of me and Jackie Sue.

Epilogue

May 1976

My fifteenth birthday party was huge. Practically everyone I knew was there—people from church, the gang from Booker and Breeze, and my friends from high school. White and Black. My parents were nervous. They seemed to think some sort of race riot was going to break out. But I finally convinced them that *my* generation didn't have all those old hang-ups.

We were all in my den dancing, eating, and laughing—Regina and Denise, Todd and Big Mouth James, Yvette and Gretchen. Church friends, school friends, B&B friends. All the different parts of my life were mingling together, having a blast. Then suddenly, in the corner of my eye I saw a face in the window. It took a minute to register, but as soon as I realized who it was, I bolted out of the den.

"Jackie Sue!" I called. "Wait!"

She turned. Catching up to her, I saw a new version of Jackie Sue Webster—a different person from the one who had walked out of my door five months earlier in a pair of my pajamas. This Jackie Sue was older, and not as sad. This one wasn't filthy. She didn't have a clump of chewed-up hair. She looked vibrant, healthy, and happy.

"Hi, Tiphanie," she said with a soft smile.

"Hey there."

"Look, I don't want to pull you away from another party. All I wanted to do was say Happy Birthday."

"Come back with me!" I told her. "At least come say hi to everyone." I took her hand in mine and tugged gently. She squeezed it before letting it go.

"No, thank you," she said. My face must have shown my disappointment, because she quickly added, "I'd love to but I can't. I have a train to catch. I'm going back to Alabama. I've gotten in touch with my aunt there, and I'm going to go live with her. My mom's living with some new boyfriend somewhere."

"What! No! Stay, Jackie Sue. Stay with us!" I said. "I have a bunch of your stuff in the garage—pictures and trophies and things from the trailer. Please come in with me. I'm sure social services would let you stay with us now, if we talked to them again."

Jackie Sue smiled and pulled me into a hug. "Thanks for the offer, but this is the best thing for me. I'm going to a place that my heart has always called home. I'll never forget you though. I'll always think of those few months we had as the Tiphanie Epoch."

I laughed softly at that. "You and those words," I said. "I'll think of it in simpler terms. The Oreo Season."

We clasped hands and stood there for a moment, knowing that the chances of our seeing each other again were slim.

Finally Jackie Sue let go. "Throw all that stuff away, Tiphanie," she said. "I don't need it anymore."

With a wave Jackie Sue turned and started walking away, heading off to find her home, a place where she'd be happy. When I couldn't see her any longer, I headed back to my house, nestled in a neighborhood where I had finally found my place.